this is not a picture

Howard David Ingham

"Why the Others Were Taken" first appeared in
A Flock of Shadows, published by Parthian Books in 2014.

"So I Caught Up With Dennis" first appeared in
The Ghastling, issue 2 (Spring 2015).

The other stories in this collection first appeared online
at CHARIOT (chariotrpg.blogspot.com)

Cover: Author/Simeon Smith

Room 207 Press

Swansea, United Kingdom

www.chariotrpg.blogspot.com

Contents

Introduction

Ekphrasis, which has always been a preoccupation of mine, is defined as the art of describing a picture in words, but it's more than that, in that the more detailed you are, the more solidly the picture ceases to become a visual thing. You pull it into the space of the imagination, transform it.

What fascinates me about the process of ekphrasis is that, as I said, by transmitting a picture into words, even if you do it right, you make it impossible to reverse engineer. Ramsey Campbell, for example, wrote "Among the Pictures Are These:" (you can find it in *Cold Print*) which is supposedly just a description of a sketchbook of his juvenile drawings, with all the obsessions of an adolescent imagination, sex and death all over it. In this piece, and all it is is a list of pictures, described one by one, the pictures move beyond the premise set and enter an imaginary space where they extend beyond simple vision. Even if they were real, and there's no reason to assume they wouldn't be, they're not now.

Virgil, in the *Aeneid*, a much more subversive work than you think it is, writes of the divinely donated Shield of Aeneas. In the area around the boss the future history of Rome from the shadowy era of myth right down to the Battle of Actium, where the gods of Rome stand behind the ships of Rome and the bestial gods of Egypt bay and slaver over the opposition.

No one could do the insane detail of the shield justice, although of course there have been attempts, because that's not its point. Ekphrasis of this imaginary object is there to extend a narrative. You almost enter the shield, and travel inside the future of the protagonist and the past for the reader, symbols that mean nothing to the eyes of its recipient, the *Aeneid's* ambivalent hero, but which recap the story of Rome, ready for the apocalyptic battles that close the poem.

MR James's ghost story "The Mezzotint" is different again. A man buys an antique engraving on a whim; it changes. As it's originally described, the picture is entirely commonplace, and could be easily duplicated, but each subsequent time the protagonist of the story sees it, it changes. Something malevolent and shapeless invades the boundaries of the static image, and again, while you could probably draw that too, the effect of the change isn't visual. The black, hunched figure that steals into the house isn't material. The very mundanity of the story's presentation casts into sharp relief the uncanny nature of the event. The picture doesn't hurt anyone. It is after all, just a picture. But it gives a picture of more than just a house; it is a picture of the supernatural.

Oscar Wilde does the opposite. He never really describes the titular *Picture of Dorian Gray* in any detail, instead understanding the effect. You can find enough detail scattered through the story to reconstruct it but Wilde is more interested in the effect of the image, its significance.

The one good film version of the story, the 1945 one with Hurd Hatfield, George Sanders and a precipitously young Angela Lansbury, does duplicate the original picture and, less successfully, the obscene final result with the marks of Dorian Gray's sins on it, and attempts to visualise the impact of both iterations of the painting by having the closeups of the painting being the only colour frames in an otherwise black and white film, which is pretty effective as it goes.

The film plays other tricks, too, beginning as an otherwise bland and innocuous period melodrama of the sort Hollywood churned out back then, and ending in a world of angular, expressionist shadows, with the bloodsoaked horror of the painting in the centre of it. It still doesn't quite hit the point, but it knows where the point is, at least. It's one of those exceptions to the rule and at any rate it's still better than the more recent, terrible version with the snarling CGI portrait and the fatally miscast Colin Firth, which is a couple of hours I'm never going to be able to recoup.

In Wilde's book, the image of the portrait, as with MR James's engraving, is only partially fluid. It changes when no one sees. The moment someone looks, it becomes a different thing. But then, by reading a written picture, so are you.

In some way or another, the response to art, to photography, to music, has been a constant preoccupation in my writing. The stories in this book were written between 2006 and 2016: every one deals in some way with writing, pictures, video, audio. The oldest piece, in which a piece of misplaced radio offers an insight into a world where horror has been normalised and life goes on, never really had a satisfying title, but it seems obvious now, in a Britain facing an uncertain and most probably bleak future, that it should be called "Leave".

"Stormboy", a set of three vignettes centred around the greatest single the Britpop era never produced, is really a tribute to a friend who died tragically young. He isn't in the story, which I suppose is the point.

"So I caught up with Dennis" (first published on the now-defunct website *Jet Pack*, and then in issue 2 of *The Ghastling*) is about friendship that died, filtered through a nightmare I had; the television screen becomes the key to the story, and it seemed only right that this happen. In "Why the others were taken", which was most recently published in Parthian Books' 2014 collection *A Flock of Shadows*, solutions come in a letter. This was a nightmare too, but it's also the truest of the stories in this collection, and in some ways the one least like the others.

"Pillar of salt" deals with a midrash, one of those strange, awkward glosses on old testament Scripture. It's in the *midrashim* you find the story of Adam's first wife, Lilith, and the strange account of Jonah giving God the finger and being swallowed by a second sea monster for his troubles. The midrash in the story isn't real, but the landmark is. "An after-hours reading" presents an idiosyncratic Tarot deck (although in some ways, all Tarot decks are idiosyncratic). The spread, twelve Minor Arcana in two rows of six, covering twelve Major Arcana, has fallen out of fashion, but was the spread favoured by Madeline Montalban, who wrote Tarot and astrology articles for *Prediction* for decades up until her death in 1983, and whose writing shaped my childhood; if the description of the Tarot reader partly recalls her and partly Madame Blavatsky, this is no coincidence.

"An envelope" is a retread of a story I wrote for a client some years ago. That original story had the dubious distinction of having been literally written in my sleep. This one tries to recapture the energy of that story, while at least this time making some sort of sense, and dispensing with the most worrying phallic imagery that story had.

8

The most recent of the stories in this collection is "*The Austringer* (1969)", which deals with a piece of lost television. It goes without saying that every one of the pieces of lost TV mentioned in the story did once exist, and most probably don't any more. The episode of *Doomwatch* where Toby Wren dies was my own father's favourite single episode of TV, and the version of it that Charlie sees is the version my father described to me, and not what you get from the shooting script. The exception, of course, is the titular ghost story, which nonetheless, I hope, is convincing as an example of the form.

By the mathematical reckoning I have a good thirty-five pictures in this little book. I hope that you enjoy them.

Howard David Ingham
Swansea, April 2017

So I caught up with Dennis

— *Some people, I say, go when they have to and whoosh, they're out of your life. But you've got that connection, right. So when you catch up again a few years later, you just pick up like right where you left off.* I pause. *You ever had that?*

— *Yeah,* she says. *Couple of people. So Dennis,* she says. *One of those people?*

— *We've met up maybe three times since uni. And each time… Memories. You know?*

She nods.

— *Do I know him?*

— *Dunno. He might've been before your time. Although. Were you at Annie's wedding?*

— *Mm-hmm.*

— *He was there. Pretty much conquered the karaoke. Little guy. Really deep voice.*

— *Oh! Yeah! With the hair, right?*

— *That's him. Guy with the hair.*

— *Oh, he was funny.*

— *Eccentric as all get out. Ha. Yeah.*

— *How long's he down for?*

— *Couple days.*

— *Lovely.*

•

I press the hang-up button, look at the phone for a minute as if anyone's texted me, out of a sort of reflex action. Dennis doesn't own a mobile.

Here's the rumble of a train; automated voices, Welsh and English, man and woman, confirming that this is indeed the train that Dennis will arrive on.

It's a little two-carriage affair. Hardly anyone is on it, and only two people get off, the first a thirtysomething woman in a business suit, good-looking enough that I feel guilty for looking at her and watching her until she has gone from the platform, and I do not see the figure in front of me, who says, in a familiar bass baritone:

— *Hello.*

I jump; I do not recognise him. He is shorter than I remember. He wears a plain black scarf wrapped around his mouth and nose. Under his battered leather jacket, he wears a wash-worn grey hoodie, and the hood is pulled up over his head. It's dark now. I have been here a long time.

— *Hello,* he says again.

His voice is always as it was, a baritone, but the kind that comes from the back of the mouth rather than the chest, which always gave the voice a kind of quiet, halting quality, emphasised by the habit he had of swallowing sometimes in mid-sentence.

— *Dennis! How are you, man?*

I put out a hand. He pauses, looks at it, shakes. His hand is very bony, very hard and very cold. A broken fingernail scrapes across the side of my hand as his grip releases.

— *I'm well. Thank you.*

I reach for the larger of his two bags.

11

— *Good journey?*

— *Fine.*

— *Shall we——?* I wave a hand towards the car.

•

— *Oh, no,* he says. *I didn't mean to give you the wrong impression. It's OK?*

I am driving.

— *Uh, yeah. Yeah. Completely.*

— *You hadn't gone to too much trouble?*

— *No. No. Not at all.* (I have let my wife and children go on holiday without me. I have cleaned the spare room from top to bottom. I have filled the fridge and freezer with vegan food.) *No. it's cool.*

We stop at a set of lights. I look across at him, wonder what is up with the scarf. Maybe it's an affectation. He's done that before, like when he went around wearing a set of NHS glasses without any glass in them. He is looking out of the passenger side window; he turns and looks at me. In the dark, he is only lit by the red light, and I cannot see his eyes. I give him a tight-lipped smile; the light changes. I return my eyes to the road, set off.

— *So whose place is it you're staying at?*

— *Joe and Sarah's. I don't think you know them.*

— *No. It doesn't ring a bell.*

— *They're not around anyway. I'm just house-sitting.*

— *Oh.*

— *It's a good base. It means I can catch up with some other people who I was wanting to see.*

— *Oh yeah? Who's that, then?*

12

— *People. You don't know them. Maybe you'll meet them on Sunday.*

— *OK.*

I drop him off at the house, one of the really big, nice places at the West Cross end of the Mumbles Road, with the really long drive and maybe six bedrooms. I would have known about someone who lived here. Wouldn't I?

He has a key.

I help him carry his bags in, look around the hall. It's beautiful. No pictures, anywhere. But lovely. Except that the cupboard door under the stair has a broken panel, the lower right-hand side one, like someone bashed a hole in it from inside with a really big hammer or something.

— *Hey,* I say. *What happened there?*

— *No idea,* says Dennis. He shuffles towards the kitchen. *Tea?*

— *Yeah.*

He watches me drink it. He doesn't have any of his own. I head back to mine. I watch TV.

•

I decided to walk. I am in no hurry, and it is already a beautiful morning. The traffic on the main road, on the other side of that wide grass verge, seems very far away. Hardly anyone else is on the esplanade, and by the time I get as far as Blackpill Lido, no one is there at all.

The beach on Swansea Bay is very wide and very flat. The tide comes in and out a mile or more in minutes, and it comes in while I walk, the sea lapping against the wall on which the south side of the path sits, that keeps Swansea from the ocean. A band of light, like a path to

13

somewhere else again, stretches across the sea from me to the still-low sun, and follows me, and I imagine hopping over the crumbling path and walking along the path, and vanishing into the light. And I would be the last to go, because everyone else has gone.

•

At the top of the drive, in front of that big white West Cross house, there's Dennis, first person I've seen today, sitting on the path next to the flower bed, hands clasped over his knees, staring at the flower bed. He's still wearing the kerchief. I stand next to him, look down, and I am a little shocked at how grey his tight brown curls have gone.

— *Hey. What are you looking at?*

He points at the earth. His finger is longer than I remember it being, the nail long and filthy, like a storybook witch. He is pointing a mass of something pinkish under and around the daffodils, a lump of something like flesh that seems to twist and fold in on itself as I watch. It takes me a moment to figure out what it is I am looking at.

— *That's an awful lot of worms,* I say.

— *Mm.*

— *What do you think they're doing?*

He doesn't reply immediately. A movement behind his kerchief reminds me of how Dennis used to lick his lips before saying something, and how you knew how he was choosing his words.

— *Did you know that there are a million earthworms for every human being on the planet?*

— *No. No, Dennis. I did not.*

— *When we're gone, they'll take over. They'll replace us.*

14

— *Wasn't that supposed to be the cockroaches?*

— *No.* He is in earnest, as he always was, serious or joking. *No, the earthworms. Definitely the earthworms.*

— *Oh.*

I put a hand in my hair, tongue in cheek, look down the path at the silent main road. I let a breath out, lower lip pushed out.

— *Listen,* I say. *Wanna do the charity shop thing?*

•

We have by this point ranged across Mumbles, West Cross and up as far as Derwen Fawr and Clyne, a circle of several miles, and we have visited shops I have never heard of, tucked away in streets I barely knew existed. The main roads are exceptionally quiet today. At times it seems like I haven't seen a single car or pedestrian, but I know for a fact I must have seen someone.

Now the side roads; I can accept that no one is there. They are dead.

The shops represent charities I have not heard of, names painted on faded board. *Indigent Support. British Asylum Builders. International Euthanasia Guild. Feed the Wretched.*

Every shop, if it appears to have anyone inside it at all, contains as its presiding spirit a single grim-faced old biddy, sitting behind a counter cluttered with porcelain knick-knacks and cheap discoloured cuddly toys, in a grotto walled with unwanted ornamental jugs and out-of-fashion clothes and jigsaw puzzles depicting seaside scenes from the other end of the country. Each time, the old woman smiles briefly at Dennis with his kerchief and shuffling gait, as he heads for the books, but fixes me with

15

an eye like a chipped glass marble, and does not look away until I have left the shop.

The smell of age hangs in my nostrils. I shift my feet. My neck itches.

By about third or maybe the fourth of these shops I start imagining things. Behind neatly folded chintz curtains and plastic baby-walkers and racks of those little old lady hats that I cannot imagine anyone makes any more, here is a foetus in formaldehyde. An electric lamp made from someone's skull, with brown twisted flex and a once-white 13 amp plug. A curved, black-handled knife, with the label in wobbly handwriting, *Sacrificial knife, 75p.*

In this last shop, a cardboard box on a chair sitting just outside the door has a sign made from one panel of a very old cornflakes packet, on which is written *FREE. Donations gratefully received within.* Dennis is already squatting by the bottom shelves, head cocked to one side, reading every spine, one by one, occasionally taking a book out, flipping through it, putting it back.

I'll wait out here, I think. Absently, I pick up a fat, tatty paperback with plain white covers, turned yellow at the spine, with the sour, decrepit smell of old cigarette smoke hanging from the paper. It falls open in my hands. I read a couple of paragraphs in which the writer discusses the best way to degrade and murder a child. I close it, without looking at the title, and put it back between *The Da Vinci Code* and some Jilly Cooper novel. I look up, see the old woman smirking through the window. Her shoulders rock gently. She is laughing at me for taking offence.

I decide to stay outside in the sun. I sit on the front garden wall of the boarded-up house next door and wait. It is beautiful today. Red-brown leaves litter this street. The sun is bright and the wind is low. It is a golden, melancholy Autumn day like the ones in which years ago I used to take solace in a comfortable kind of loneliness, or in friends like Dennis and the collections we shared, whiling away the time until I was no longer single, no longer without children.

I cannot hear traffic anywhere.

As Dennis comes out of the shop, he slips something whitish and I think evil-looking into his jute shopping bag. He sits on the wall next to me. It surprises me a little how small he is. How his feet dangle next to the ground.

— *Find what you were after?* I say.

— *Some things.*

I run a hand through my hair, let out one of those sighs that sometimes used to serve when I was younger as a conversational gambit, when I was uncomfortable with nothing being said. The breeze turns cold.

— *You know,* I say. *I don't think I've ever seen Mumbles so dead. We've barely seen a soul.*

Dennis grunts. It's an odd, wet noise, as if made around the base of the tongue and rolled around before coming out. His kerchief moves a little. I put my hands on my knees, turn to look at him. It is late in the afternoon and the sun is in my eyes. I cannot clearly see his face.

— *Dennis,* I say. *I have to ask.*

He makes a throat-clearing sound.

— *Hmm?*

— *You know your* — I wave my fingers around in front of my mouth — *I was wondering why you were wearing it. I mean, it's not like the glasses. Is it?*

— No. It's not like the glasses.

— OK. So, can I ask — ?

— Do you remember, he says, *where you were twenty-three, perhaps, and you said…you said you felt how if you were in trouble… or felt trapped. That you did not have to stay. Anywhere. That there would always be a way out? You remember.*

— I remember. It was a long time ago. I don't —

— You were wrong.

He is looking away from me, toward the sun. He is unsteady in his posture, swaying, not solid. For a moment, against my will, I imagine that he is not my old friend, but that he is a double made from hundreds of worms, and that I could poke him and he will disintegrate into a wave of worms that would wriggle and slither away from an emptying heap of clothes.

— I was young, I say. *You say things like that when you're young. Because you have to. Because when you're that age you think you're invincible. And you wouldn't achieve anything if you didn't.*

He clears his throat again. As has always been Dennis' way.

I stand.

— Where to next? I say.

Dennis hops down, smooths his hands on his cords as if they are wet or dirty. He gestures up the hill.

— One more. It's just around the corner.

•

— So, I say, *are they on holiday or something?*

We are standing in the hall of the big West Cross house and I am hanging up my jacket on a brass wall hook.

— *Something like that,* says Dennis.

I got a bag of chips at Dick Barton's. Dennis said he wasn't hungry. He never ate much, I tell myself. He sorts me out with a plate and fork, and watches me.

But I admit to myself a faint disappointment that I shall not see him eat. I'll walk home, I say. I should start soon, I say. Maybe I'll be in time for the last bus, I say. Tomorrow, I say?

— *Not in the daytime,* he replies. *I promised a few people I'd catch up with them.*

— *But in the evening. Film and* Who?

— *I would like that.*

— *Tomorrow night, then. Maybe,* I say, giving in to my curiosity, *you can get your mysterious mates along.*

— *Maybe.*

•

A bus pulls up at the stop before the roundabout. The 3A, my bus. Its doors open and the driver turns his head towards me.

He looks like he's made of earthworms, thousands of them all knotted together, writhing, imperfectly forming and reforming eyes and lips as worms wriggle away into the mass and new ones take their places. Overflowing from and wriggling back into a filthy FirstBus Cymru uniform. No one else is on the bus.

I step back, as you do; the uniform shrugs and shudders. A pulpy hand presses the button, closes the door. The bus moves on. I shake my head. I'm tired. It's dark.

19

I shall walk home.

•

I spend most of Sunday at home. I catch up on my reading. I walk along the seafront as the sun sets.

I don't see or hear from a living soul all day.

•

On the massive flatscreen television that would consume the wall of any other house, but which looks in place here, Tom Baker runs in that somewhat sedate way 1970s British actors do through a corridor, pursued by marching aliens in round helmets. My eyes grow heavy. He runs through the TARDIS. He runs through a public swimming baths. I drop off.

I wake up; still in the lounge of that big West Cross house, and the room is dark and the TV is still on, and now Dennis and I have company, six or seven others perched on a footstool, the sofa, the floor. The lights are down. Their faces are in shadow. They're all watching the TV. It takes me a minute for my eyes to get used to the dark.

Every face is covered, every figure is small and skinny, mostly male as far as I can tell, although one wears a floral dress and black tights, without having any other sign of gender. Every one has his or her face covered, at least in the lower half. A huge Tom Baker woolly scarf, wrapped up round and round over a nose. A hockey mask, or something like a hockey mask, not like the bloke in the horror film, more modern than that. A black bandana, printed with skulls and roses and thorns and 1980s rock band images. Someone sitting on the floor near the door, peering through the gap between the sofa and the armchair in which I am sitting, is wearing a motorcycle helmet.

20

Here is Dennis, on the other side of the room, sitting on the arm of the big armchair by the bay window. It is hard to see, but I am convinced that he glances at me and sees that I am awake, and nods towards the TV screen. I squint into the dark, trying to make out these people. Did Dennis introduce me to his friends? Was I so tired I don't even remember?

Someone on the TV screams.

On screen, a corpse, the big reveal. A young son and a teenage daughter have found their father, his face eaten off, one of his arms missing, and they are sick with shock and fear. They hold each other, mouth reassurances, and it becomes apparent, though it is not spelled out, that these words have long ago become unfamiliar to them.

They are in the kitchen now, and they begin to again. They do not know what to do. The girl is begging her brother to take a carving knife; he is near-hysterical. The boy runs to the lounge, tries to curl up behind the sofa. The girl chases him, sits on the floor beside him. She tries to calm him down, stops shouting, holds the boy tight, tells him, perhaps for the first time in a very long time, that she loves him, that everything will be all right.

The lights go out.

The girl holds her brother tight, and then slowly, they get up. She takes her brother's hand, and tells him to be quiet. They advance to back of the house. They keep to the wall. The girl holds the knife out in front of her. They get to the back door. It is locked. The key is just there, across the kitchen. She puts her finger to her lips and smiles, and leaves the boy at the back door as she crosses the kitchen, walking around the wall of the room. She puts out her hand to get the key from its hook.

Something stiff and strangely apelike reaches down from above the cooker and grabs her, lifts her kicking and screaming from the floor and up out of shot. Cut to a close-up of the knife dropping to the kitchen floor and clattering, and drops of blood, first one or two and then great splatters, falling on it. The screams continue.

The boy snaps and runs past the falling blood, back into the house, dives into the cupboard under the stairs, closes the door, curls into a ball.

Cut to his face, streaked with tears. He tries his absolute best to collect himself, not altogether successfully, and it is then we see something terrible dawn upon him. He is not breathing raggedly; the sound of panting continues. The camera pans up from his face. Behind him and above him we see a grinning maw, full of those broad stained, uneven teeth. They part. A long pointed tongue licks around a huge lipless mouth.

Cut again: a simple view of the cupboard door under the stairs, central on screen. The handle moves once, twice. Something inside bangs against the door. A brief scream, muffled. The lower right-hand panel of the door buckles suddenly from the inside with a single loud crack, like it had a smart impact from a sledgehammer, or if someone kicked it really, really hard. Then silence.

The credits roll over the shot of the door.

And I think, *wait*. The small smothered figures around me watch intently, silently as the names of actors I have never heard of roll up the screen and it fades to black. They have all moved slightly closer to the screen. I am no longer sure which one is Dennis. My eyes are so, so heavy. I am warm. I am not, I register with sleepy surprise, frightened. I nod off.

It is full morning and I am lying on the sofa with a crick in my neck. The plush upholstery is damp under my face, where I have drooled on it. Someone has draped a blanket over me.

The bay window faces south and slightly east, and although the curtains are closed, the room is filled with soft golden light. Dennis is sitting on the arm of the chair nearest the bay window. By the time I have seen him, he has turned away. He stands, steps to the side of the bay, pulls the cord. The curtains open with a sort of hiss.

Bright sunlight fills the room. Dennis approaches. I sit up, hand on the back of my neck, the thumb and index finger of my other hand on my eyelids. I put my hands on my knees, blink, squint into the light. Dennis stands almost in silhouette in front of me.

— *Sleep well?* he says.

I make a non-committal sort of noise. My eyes get used to the light. Dennis is not wearing his kerchief.

The lower half of Dennis' face is wholly taken up by his grinning moon-on-its-side mouth, vast and wide, chipped teeth like piss-streaked gravestones. The gums are bordered by choppy scar tissue as if someone cut the lips off with a Stanley knife to make room for the mouth. A slightly raised area of reddish flesh, dotted with blackheads, sits where a nose should be. His eyes are perfectly round, sit under heavy, low brows, and are indeterminate in number: one, two, more, I can't tell.

And Dennis' voice.

— *Cup of tea?*

I screw up my eyes again, try to squeeze the picture out of my head, open them, look straight at him. Teeth. Eyes. Ruined flesh.

— *Yes. That would be nice.*

So we head to the kitchen, past the cupboard door with the wrecked panel, and we sit at the kitchen table, me and the old friend with the charnel mouth, and he makes me a cup of Earl Grey, and I am stiff and shivering and I am breathing irregularly with little yelps like I'm about to hyperventilate, or already am hyperventilating, only I haven't realised that I am yet. He watches as my hands shake and I fight to raise the mug to my lips and drink, and I think I spill some, and Dennis show no sign that he has noticed. He watches with no drink of his own, hands clasped on the table, grinning, grinning, grinning.

And he says to me, after a time,

— *It's been really good to see you, Simon.*

I put the mug down.

— *Yeah. Thanks.*

— *I thought of you often.*

— *Yeah. I did, too.* I realise that this is true.

— *I used to count you as one of the best friends I had ever had.* He sounds terribly sad. He grins. *I was so glad when we caught up. It's been great catching up. It has.*

I nod. He clears his throat.

— *It means a lot that you would come to visit me,* he says.

And this makes no more sense than the face. I know I should reply with yes, great, let's do it again sometime, but I cannot, and it dawns on me that perhaps Dennis knows full well that I cannot, and that he approves of my honesty.

24

— You're still one of my oldest and best friends. I hope you know that, he says.

I am facing the hall. I can see the door to the cupboard under the stairs.

— I do, I say. *We have history, don't we?*

•

I shake his hand, which is cold and hard and lumpy and which has appallingly long nails. I do not offer to accompany him back to the train station, because I think I would be unable to keep from guessing what train he will take, and where it will go, and I don't think that I could cope with that.

So we say goodbye, and although it has begun to drizzle, I ignore the bus stop, and I cross the still-silent Mumbles Road by the West Cross Inn, and walk along the esplanade and watch the tide come in and grow whiter and angrier. By the time I rejoin the main road a good hour later, I have to press the button on the Pelican crossing at the bottom of Brynmill Lane and wait for the green man because the road is too busy to cross without waiting.

I walk up the hill, passing the usual traffic of young mums and hungover students and pensioners The seagulls and swans are in fine voice across the lake at Brynmill Park, angry and hungry and declaring that they are alive, they are alive.

And I unlock the door, and pick up a letter for my wife from the bank and a Jiffy bag containing a Scott Walker CD I won off of eBay last week. And I sit in my lounge and let the cat come and sit by me, and I absent-mindedly stroke him, and I wonder what I am going to tell my wife, when she brings my young son home and asks me, *how was your weekend?*

Why the others were taken

— *You have to understand,* says my father, *that your grandmother was not a bad woman. She saw a lot of tragedy in her life.*

My father is standing in his sitting room holding an open Tupperware box, in which he has deposited broken bits of cheesy Quaver, limp white cucumber and lettuce sandwiches, abandoned party-size sausage rolls harvested from the coffee table and the settee. Beyond practical arrangements for the funeral, this is the first opinion that Dad has expressed regarding his mother-in-law since I got back here.

My father's house — I grew up here — I stopped thinking about it as "home" a long time ago — has been more or less silent for half an hour. Now that the wake is over, we are making the house presentable again.

Dad doesn't have a dishwasher. My hands are red and a bit wrinkly. I have splashed water on my dress. I came back in to ask him where the salad bowls go. The cupboards are all arranged differently now. I haven't lived here for a long time.

I put the glass bowl down on the coffee table. I can't think of an appropriate response. He's been crying. I have never seen him cry and it takes a moment to recognise it — the red eyes, the shininess on the cheeks.

— *Dad,* I say.

I know he isn't crying for Nan.

Bang. The sound of a fist on the front door echoes through the house. Dad stiffens. It comes again, bang, and he looks away from me, face contorted. A third time: bang. A fourth: bang. Four more: bang, bang, bang, bang.

— *I'll get that,* I say.

Four more again: bang, bang, bang, bang.

— *No,* he says. *I think I'd rather you didn't.*

•

The last time I had spoken properly to my Nan was on the day of my mother's funeral. This was six months ago. I had been up to talk to her a few times already, and I had told her how sorry I was that her daughter — not my mother, her daughter — had died so suddenly. She had been dismissive and cold. I had brought her several cups of tea; she had not thanked me. I had come to offer to drive her to Mum's funeral, to push the wheelchair; she had refused.

I had left her sitting up in bed in her room at the top of my parents' stairs, staring at the gaps in the yellow wallpaper on the wall opposite, hand clasped in her lap like a little heap of kindling. I had stood at the lectern in the Chapel of Rest and had read the fourteenth chapter of John's Gospel to the assembled mourners: *In my house are many rooms. If it were not so, I would have told you. I go now to prepare a place for you.* I imagined Nan, the whole time, in the bed, scowling into space.

After the burial, when I returned, she was still in that position. I said, *Hello, Nan,* and she didn't move, so I repeated myself, and she said, without looking at me,

— *I 'eard you the first time, maid.*

— *How are you, Nan?*

— *How d'ye bleddy think I am, ye bleddy fool?*

I bit my lip. I rested my hand on the back of my neck, looked down at a stain on the carpet.

— *Nan,* I said, *Uncle Derek is here. He wanted to come and see you.*

She stared at the wall.

— *Derek, Nan.*

She sucked on her lips for a moment.

— *'E can pess right off.*

— *Nan-*

— *No, 'e had his chance. 'e coulda come back any time. Too late for 'im now. Too late. 'E can't come back begging now. 'Ee en't tekken any more from me, you 'ear me? He can pess right off. Tell him to pess off, maid.*

I wanted to hit her. I wanted to say, get yourself a sense of proportion, you evil old baggage. I wanted to say, it should be you who died. I said,

— *All right.*

And I went downstairs, and I left Dad to deal with her, and three days later I went home without once opening the door at the top of the stairs or saying goodbye.

And the day after I went home, Nan had the first of a dozen or more minor strokes, and her mind and the last of her control over her body went, in the space of a week. Dad, denied the time to mourn Mum, spent the next six months nursing her. I wondered sometimes if Nan was punishing him for loving her daughter.

•

When the echo of the knocks has subsided, Dad sits down on the table, holding the plastic box on his lap, and presses the thumb and first finger of one hand into his eyes. He sighs.

The he snaps to, puts the box on the table, stands off, walks out of the room.

— *I'm making tea,* he says. He heads to the kitchen.

I follow.

— *Dad,* I say, *What just happened?*

— *It's probably just kids.*

— *So what, it's happened before?*

— *Every so often, yes.*

— *And you never answered it?*

— *No.*

— *Oh, good grief. How long has this been going on, Dad?*

— *Since your mother went. Two or three times a week.*

— *Have you called the police or anything?*

— *No. They just bang on the door. Nothing ever happens. No does anything.*

He's shaking. Some of the tea spills on the worktop.

— *Oh, Dad.*

I leave it for a moment. Then, I try to sit him down with his tea while I finish the tidying. He isn't having any of it.

•

Nan had been in the bed in Mum and Dad's spare room for about a year — there was no question of being able to afford a place in a home — when Mum re-established contact with Uncle Derek. She never told me how, just that it was an accident, a coincidence. In the space of a minute, an older brother Mum had not seen for fifty years stumbled, politely apologising, back into her life.

Mum had gone, still in tears, to tell her mother that she had just seen Derek, and Nan had said, So what? And Mum had said, *But it's Derek,* and Nan had said that what is buried and dead must remain buried and dead.

Nan lived by that phrase, or claimed to.

•

— *It was good of Derek to come,* I say. *After... everything.*

— *He couldn't do any less.* Dad puts his mug down. He grew up using tea leaves and even though he's used teabags for years, he always leaves a bit at the bottom.

— *He'd have been justified in not coming.*

— *It was his duty. It doesn't matter what she did. She was his mother.*

— *I thought she wasn't to blame for what happened.*

— *Oh, your Nan had her part.*

I am surprised for a moment at the depth of feeling in my father's statement, that he, a man so cautious, so softly spoken, so unwilling to speak ill of the dead, especially the dead, might be able today of all days to say something about that vile old woman that is true.

— *So what actually happened, Dad?*

He leans over and picks up the mug, looks into it, puts it down, looks at me. His fingers twitch like he is about to light a cigarette, but he gave up years ago, so he looks uncomfortable and licks his lips and says,

— *Well.*

And then the banging on the door starts again.

•

At some time during the Second World War, when my mother was barely even walking, all of her four older brothers and sisters were taken away by the Social, and put into an orphanage.

Mum was an evacuee. During the Blitz, she was sent to the country, and when the bombing raids were over, she came back home to a home she was too young to have remembered the first time, and to the first of three younger siblings. Before her evacuation, she was the youngest of five; now she was the eldest of four. Her mother was not even thirty when the youngest was born.

When they had come of age, the four elder children, now grown, came back. They argued with their parents and bullied my mother, and then, as soon as each found some place to go, one by one they went away and did not come back, and only they and my grandparents knew why this had happened. But they had gone away, and Nan and Grandad would not ever speak of the others again, or even admit that they had existed.

•

Bang. Bang. Bang. Bang.

Dad puts out a hand, but I am on my feet and sprinting for the door and I am furious, ready to thump someone. I snatch the key off the hook and fumble with the lock and ball my fists and draw in breath ready to scream abuse at my father's tormentor.

The smell hits me in the face, stops me in my tracks. I recoil, back of my hand to my mouth, eyes immediately watering.

The figure on the doorstep judders; clods of earth fall on to the doorstep. I do not recognise her. Dad is behind me; I did not notice him there. He pushes next to me and says, in a small, sad voice,

— *Moira?*

For a moment, I wonder who Moira is, if my father knew *another* Moira. Dad says the name again. And I choke and hold my gorge down as it comes to me.

— *Mum,* I say.

Dad is leaning on me. He is swaying. I put my arm around him, prop him up.

And then Mum, six months dead and standing on my doorstep, with the earth of the grave on the tattered dress and her fingertips ripped and bloodied, with the little mole on the side of her nose and the two rings on the third finger of her left hand... Mum begins to scream.

I am unable to move beyond supporting the near-dead weight of my father, and it is his weight that brings back to myself, and my mum stops screaming. She judders again. More earth thuds to the ground, explodes on the doorstep.

The head turns a fraction, and eyes the colour of month-old milk stare at me. She opens her mouth, as if to speak. Nothing comes out apart from a wet rattle.

Dad straightens up, draws in breath. He pushes me gently to one side and takes Mum's hand gently in his, leads her past me. She stumbles, rights herself, drags one foot. Dad leads her inside into the lounge. I look up and down the street and shut the door.

— *She's cold,* says Dad. *She's really cold.*

He sends me upstairs to get a blanket. I stare at him for a minute, but I cannot think of anything else to do, so I go, and soon Mum is sat on the sofa with a blanket around her and we are at a loss as to what to do next.

We sit with Mum until dawn, and she says nothing, and stares into space, and sometimes she rattles. The lights are all on, but the corners of the room seem very dark.

•

At about nine in the morning, I make some tea. I am not thinking. I pour four cups, put three of them onto a tray, take them into the lounge, turn to go back into the kitchen.

— *I was just* — I stop myself.

— *What?* says Dad.

— *I made another cup. For* — *I was going to take it to* — I shake my head.

Dad is staring at me.

Making sure not to look at the door at the top of the stairs, I return to the kitchen, pour it down the sink.

Mum doesn't drink hers. When it has cooled down a little, Dad tries to get her to drink some by holding the cup to her mouth, but it trickles out the sides.

— *Right,* says Dad. *This can't go on. She's smells awful. She's filthy.*

It's the damp metallic sort of smell that earth has, the smell that grits up the back of your throat, a taste that reminds you of things you would never willingly eat, like mould and earthworms, all mixed in with something else, something unfamiliar and queasy. She smells like she's crawled out of the ground.

What can we do? We lead her upstairs and we give her a bath. I leave Dad to undress her — I can't, she's my Mum

33

— but it's up to me to pick her up like a baby and lift her into the water. She is very light. Fragile and awkward, like an armful of swept-up leaves. I keep expecting her to fall apart in my hands. When she hits the water, she begins to scream again. Dad steadies himself on the door frame, turns, stumbles, falls to his knees on the landing, vomits on the carpet.

— *Dad?* I don't know if I should leave Mum or go to him. I try to call out over the screaming. *Dad, are you OK?*

He is already on his feet and heading for the stairs. Mum stops screaming.

— *I'm going to get some disinfectant and a bucket,* he says.

I turn to Mum and start to try to clean her up. Her teeth are yellow. Her skin is greyish and pockmarked with deep, bloodless, ragged holes. And out of those sour-milk eyes leak viscous white tears.

I can see a snail floating in the bath.

I reach in and take Mum's hand, lift it, stroke it gently.

— *It's all right, Mum. It's OK. It's all going to be fine.*

She turns and looks at me with those terrible opaque eyes, mouth hanging open. She rattles again.

— *Mum?*

And she rattles again. Dad comes back in. Mum looks up at him. Her hands splash feebly in bath as she does so.

— *Dad, I think she knows.*

— *Oh, God,* he says. *Oh, God. Moira?*

She begins to scream again.

•

My mother, now cleaned up and dressed in clothes my Dad could never bring himself to give to a charity shop or throw away like he said he had, is lying on the couch. Dad is perched on the end, stroking her forehead the way he used to when she had a migraine. Occasionally, she rattles and twitches.

When the phone rings, she starts again to scream, until Dad takes her hand and whispers soothingly to her. I head to the kitchen to get it.

It's Derek.

— *Is your Dad there, Jan?*

— *Um, he's sort of busy. Can I take a message?*

— *No, I can tell you. It's probably better I tell you. You're blood.*

— *What's wrong?*

— *Well, nothing. Everything. Listen. I don't know you so well, but you're Moira's. And that matters. I wanted to say goodbye. That's all.*

I say nothing. He can hear me breathing.

— *I tried. To put things right with Mother — your grandmother, I mean* — He tails off.

— *I understand,* I say.

— *Yes, I think you do. I had to do right by her. At the funeral. But.*

I know where this is going.

— *I am sorry I couldn't say earlier, Jan. To be honest, I have only just decided. I owe it to you and Eric to tell you.*

35

For a second, I want to say to him, *Let me put Mum on,* but I know that's insane, and it would damage him, damage his own grief, not only for his sister but for his life.

— *I never told your mother why, Jan.*

Decades of hurt, several generations' worth. And it all boils down to that one little why.

— *I wrote a letter,* he says. *I never gave it to her. I want you to have it. You won't have to read it if you don't want to. But—*

— *I know,* I say.

— *I think it's better if we cut off contact now. I don't have anything against you. I just think I need to draw a line under that part of my life.*

— *I understand,* I say. *It was a privilege to meet you, Uncle Derek.*

— *I am not sure that you're right. Still, I've sent it now. I don't know. Maybe it should have been buried.*

The hairs on the back of my neck stand up. I suddenly become aware that I am not alone in the kitchen. I am very cold. I do not turn around. I fix my gaze to the little orange display on the phone cradle.

— *I know,* I say.

I imagine a hand touching my shoulder.

— *Good luck, Jan. Send my regards to your father.*

I will not turn around.

— *Goodbye, Uncle Derek. And thank you.*

He hangs up. I put the receiver back on the cradle and I stand there silently, transfixed, my hand still on the receiver—

36

I whirl around. It's eleven in the morning, but the kitchen is dark. The shadows spread, even as I watch, from the corners of the room, leak around the edges.

I swallow.

I walk slowly to the sink, and I fill the kettle and I put it on, and I make a pot of tea. By the time I leave the kitchen with two mugs of tea, I can feel the shadows brushing against my skin, like the frail, paper-dry fingers of someone very old.

I stop at the bottom of the stairs, look up. The door to Nan's room is so covered in shadows it cannot be seen at all.

•

I don't know how long we've been here now, Dad and me, sitting here next to Mum, me on the floor, Dad still perched on the couch. It feels like days. We haven't slept or washed. Neither of us has eaten anything substantial apart from a few leftovers. We have up to now subsisted on tea and biscuits, but the milk is running out, and we finished the last of the biscuits, even the Rich Teas, some time ago. It's so dark in here. All the lights are on.

Neither of us has any idea what time it is. We have an unspoken, irrational agreement not to open the curtains, and it is unclear to me whether that is to keep people outside from seeing in or to keep us seeing what might be outside. We might have sat through a second night. Maybe even a third. We don't know.

When the letterbox goes, we're both surprised. Neither of us thought it was morning.

— *One of us should get that,* says Dad.

— *Yeah,* I say.

— *Jan,* says Dad, *I don't think I can.*

— *It's OK, Dad.*

Mum rattles.

I stand up and take a breath. I step into the shadows. They paw at me weakly, breathe on me with a smell like old cabbage and cigarettes and poverty. They are only shadows.

The hall stretches in front of me for miles. I cannot see the front door. Just Dad's tatty, faded carpet. Just Dad's magnolia walls, fading into the distance, into the dark.

— *I don't care, Nan,* I say out loud. *I don't care.*

And now I am sitting on the doormat with my back against the front door with a handful of post: a condolence card from someone I have never heard of; a bank statement; a charity mass-mailer, the sort where they include the cheap ballpoint pen so you have no excuse but to fill in the form; and a letter addressed to Mum. I drop the rest of the post on the floor and look at it in both hands. The shadows snake out of the air and try to snatch it from me, but they are just shadows. I pick it up, unopened, and return to the lounge through the frustrated dark.

When I reach Dad and Mum, I open the letter and say, *This is for you, Mum,* and I begin to read it to her, and before I have finished she is screaming again. Dad has his hands clamped over his ears.

It is long. It explains everything. The room gets darker as I read it. I do not stop. When I finish, Mum's screams subside to a constant rattling, which rises and subsides in waves, which has the rhythm of something sobbing.

The darkness stretches forward, threatens to engulf us all completely.

I walk into it, and I run up the stairs three steps at a time, and I stand outside Nan's door and I call in:

— *We know, Nan! We know what happened. We know why. We know why, Nan, and I don't care. Stop punishing us for this. It happened thirty years before I was born, Nan. Derek's moved on. It's nothing to do with Dad any more. No one else is alive who cares, Nan. Stop punishing us. And stop punishing Mum, Nan. No one cares. Do you hear me? No one cares!*

I am crying out at the top of my voice, and I stop only when inside the room I hear crashes and bangs, the sounds of splintering wood and smashing glass. The door bangs as something hits it hard from the other side, and then it stops and there is silence, and the house is in daylight again.

But the screaming continues downstairs, and I realise that this time it's Dad.

When I get to the lounge door the smell, worse than ever, assaults me, and across the sofa is something made of mud and slime and bones and disintegrating, worm-ridden meat, and Dad stops screaming and straightens up and he has parts of my mother's decaying flesh all down his front, over his hands and up his arms, and he has tears streaming down his face, and he is yelling at me in a broken, shrill voice: *What did you do? What did you do?*

An envelope

I was out looking for Bethan again. I do it more than ever now. Like a couple of times a month. I mean, not that I am actually looking for her, or that I expect to bump into her or something. But I look. It's like a compulsion, a need. I go walking. Looking for Bethan.

Just walking. Along the seafront. Around the roundabout at the end of Bryn Road with the old people's home on it. Where they found the car. Same route every time.

Just walking. I was done, actually on my way home, on the front, past the rec on the St. Helen's side, must have been about nine in the evening. And I wasn't really in the world. Just letting the traffic whizz by and the wind blow in my face and thinking about getting over it.

Looking for Bethan. I don't expect to see anyone or talk to anyone. I was preoccupied. Someone walked by me on the side nearer the road and said something, and I said, "Sorry, what?" without even thinking. I remember wondering for a moment if I knew him.

I'd never seen him before. And he stopped and turned and looked at me, and then he was right in my face. Young, right, but with this red, cracked skin all around his mouth and his nostrils and this smell. Like poverty: all cigarettes and sweat. His breath in little clouds, puff, puff, puff, every one vile, pungent.

"Sorry," I said. I sped up. I moved on. He overtook me, stood in front of me, barred my way.

I think I looked around then. Like I was appealing to the traffic.

No one was going to stop. And then as if he hadn't even moved it, his hand was on my throat and I could see that one of his eyes was all white and milky, like it had a cataract, and he slapped me with the other hand, like a girl would slap me, and my glasses fell off. He said he wanted my money. I didn't have any. Something coiled up, tight as a fist in my stomach.

I had my hands around his wrist. He said he was drunk. I began to hate him.

And me. I hated me. The ease with which he had me. The way I started begging for him to go away. He started laughing at me. I don't recall properly what happened then, at least not in any order.

I kicked him in the shin. His grip loosened. He swore and he tried to hit me again, but he was off-balance and missed an easy shot at me. I batted his hand off my throat and struck out, and somehow connected with his throat with some force and he sort of gurgled, and he was on the pavement and then I started kicking him and screaming at him and then there was blood and he wasn't moving, and I was standing by him with my stomach all knotted up and my hands shaking. I picked up my glasses from the ground, thankfully intact, and the wallet that had fallen from my pocket, my house keys, and without thinking, scooped up what looked like a small white envelope that had fallen on the ground next to him. And then I stood in the dark, hot and shivering, with my breath in small urgent clouds, and looked over my shoulder at the traffic whizzing past. No one was on the street. None of the cars paid any notice of me.

And I stood there shaking for a minute, in the wide open air, and then I started to run, and I ran until I got home and sank to the floor in my coat with my back to the front door, and realised only then that what I was holding was not mine, an unsealed envelope, in which I found a handful of photographs, Polaroids.

Each one had on the white part below the photo a number scrawled in permanent marker, from one to nine.

One:

A picture of Swansea Station, Platform Two, from a vantage point near the exit. The shoulder and arm of what looks like a policeman, judging by details of the uniform, can be seen on the left-hand edge of the picture. A line of people, standing behind each other, are queuing to get onto a train. They're very thin. Their clothes are in rags. You can't see their faces, but from the backs of their hairless heads they are small and you can see something is very wrong with them.

It is like — as far as you can tell, because they are some distance away and the focus is blurry they're really small — their hairless heads are covered with scabs, or scales. The Cross-Country train — one of the newer kind of train — looks very old, its paint cracked and covered with graffiti, the visible metal rusted or filthy. From inside the near-opaque windows you can see a light, and if you look very closely, one person inside, his or her face and hands pressed against the window, his scream a small black smear.

I think I spent hours just looking at them, one after the other. Each one shows part of town, but it's *wrong*, like there's something in the place of a building, or a street, or a landmark each time, or the building is somehow different, or the people are wrong. That something hideous is always present, even if it might not be directly visible. All in the washed-out colours of a faded Polaroid.

I thought — I don't know. I thought that they might be fakes to start with. I mean, they were so odd. I thought that someone might have done them for fun. Or for an art project or something. These are Polaroids, right. Old ones. I thought they were really hard to fake.

Two:

This is Brynmill. By the Rhyddings. The sun is big, and bright, and red and terribly close, and it creates a flare in the lens, washes everything with red. The windows of the pub are all cracked; the one car visible, a Mini, parked on the corner, is a burnt-out wreck. At the corner of the shot, where the school crossing could be, someone out of shot is holding the Children Crossing lollipop sign; only the wizened, blackened hand is visible.

I lived in fear for a few days, half expecting the police to knock on the door, or for something to appear in the Evening Post. But nothing happened, no consequences.

I kept the pictures in a drawer in my old bureau, and I think I looked at them about five, six, seven times a day. Just leafing through them, wondering why they had been made like that.

I couldn't figure out how they did it. I mean, you can do a lot with CGI these days, but it only looks like something other than computer graphics when you have millions and millions to put into a studio. And then only about ten per cent of the time, maybe.

I tried Googling it. It's easy enough, if you're talented, to make a picture and mess with the colours so they look like a Polaroid. But the paper. The black stuff on the back. The texture of the white material that frames it. Why would you fake that? How could you?

I thought about taking them to Collier's, maybe, to see what they thought, but then I thought that I might have to explain how I got them. And so I put them away and then I took them out, over and over.

Three:

This is the bowling green on Brynmill Park. In the middle of the picture, a man is on fire. He is on his knees and his arms are outstretched towards the camera, beseeching the photographer, and his face is contorted in agony. He is surrounded by three policemen, standing, doing nothing. One, on the right, is holding a can of petrol. On the left, one of the policemen has turned to look at the camera. Even though he is facing you, you cannot see his face. At the very edge of the picture, where the pavilion should be, you can see the corner of a building made of black stone that shines in the sunlight.

I began to think about the pictures all the time. And the more I looked at them, the more I started to fantasise about them, to imagine if they were real.

And then I started thinking about Bethan. And then I started to wonder why I was thinking about Bethan, why on earth the pictures brought her of all people to mind, she who never even watched a horror movie in her life. And I pored over the photographs even more, trying to see something hidden in them, as if they could tell me where she went, as if they were a clue to where she had gone.

I can't stop thinking about her. Where she is. What she's doing. Whether I should send her a text, or try to call again. I cannot stop myself thinking about her. My thoughts are not my own.

Four:

This is Pantygwydr Road, seen from the bottom of the hill. The sky is that same washed-out blue of the Polaroid high-summer, but the houses all look derelict, and the cars are burned out, and the trees that line the avenue seem to be made of something other than wood, and reach sinuous branches to the sky like fingers. One tree, in the foreground to the left, has snared a bird in its tendrils, a seagull, its beak wide open, looking for all the world as if it is, although doomed, struggling to escape.

I am being watched. If you like, you can check out the window. Without it looking like it's obvious. They're there. I know they are. In a rusty old black Vauxhall Astra. Two of them. Old men, in these filthy suits. Yes, them. They've been following me around for maybe four or five days now.

A few days later, I went back. To where the car was found. And around the corner to where the fight was. I passed the old people's home on the roundabout at the end of Bryn Road. All the way there I kept seeing this rusted up black Astra. And at some point it dawned that they were following me. It wasn't even subtle. I turned and looked at them, and these two old men in filthy suits stared at me with pale, watery old-man eyes and didn't look away.

They followed me home and parked outside my house. And every time I went out, they followed me. Not saying or doing anything. Parked on the corner, just looking at me with those sad, tired eyes.

I shivered, crossed the road as if to talk to them. They started the car, and rounded the corner. I belted around the corner. I could not see them, nor hear the engine. Only the silence of the evening and the sound of the sea. And then I started thinking about Bethan again.

Five:

This is somewhere in Sketty, I think. It looks like the church on the crossroads, taken from the middle of the roundabout. The bell tower, under a deep purple sky, has split open, cracked from the top, widening; in the maw it creates are neat rows of long, white teeth.

It was a couple of evenings after that. I was walking home from work. I stopped about halfway, and stared at a back lane I had just passed. Perfectly normal. Except that in a year of walking along this street I had never passed it, twenty yards past the other lane that I did recognise, and which I had already crossed. Moss between concrete paving slabs. Ivy on decaying red-brick walls. Bin bags behind rusting garage doors. And then I walked back to the other lane, two houses away. No different. And then I counted the house numbers: 34, 36, lane. 38, 40, lane, 46. Two houses missing.

And the second time I came back to the "new" lane, the men came. The old men from the car. In these threadbare, ragged suits, with runny eyes and scabs on their faces. And one of them tried to grab me, and drag me down the alley, and his mate went for my other arm, and I pulled away easily and fell right out of the alley, flat on my face on the pavement.

I flipped myself over, sitting on the ground, and in front of me was a house. Lights on. Number 44. I know. I think I'm going mad.

Six:

The Quadrant bus station is the only building on a vast, empty plain, no sign of its neighbours anywhere to be seen; between us and the building, a rocky chasm; it looks like a cathedral. Something is standing behind it, something vast, something with huge long feathery fingers that curl around the building's roof. It is in shadow, silhouetted by the redness of the sun. Its face is cut off by the top of the image.

I went straight home and got drunk. It occurred to me — no, listen — that they are real photos. Real photos of Swansea. Like there is more to the places built here.

Like they are photographs of terrain that sits in the cracks between the landmarks we know. We fool ourselves that distance are concrete, but it might not be that way. You could look to one side and suddenly find yourself looking at different landmarks completely.

I could take a wrong turn down a back lane like that one I nearly got pulled down and never find my way back again.

Seven:

Fabian Way. Just before Amazon Park. Broad daylight again. Two rusted, burned out cars sit abandoned on the side of the road in the foreground, and inside one is something indistinct, hairy, that looks like an animal. On the bonnet of the car is a human arm, torn off at the elbow, end of the bone visible in a ring of ruined flesh. You can see flowers tattooed on the skin.

I had a phone call from Bethan's mother yesterday. She was crying and angry, like nearly hysterical. It took me a while to get out of her what had happened.

47

Someone — some nutter, she said — had put a letter through her door, all handwritten, like Bethan's handwriting, only all shaky, like someone had faked it. Did she know who had done it? There was almost an accusatory note in her voice. Did she still have it? I said. I told her I'd go round and look at it.

She didn't offer me a cup of tea.

She always blamed me. As if, as if, as if. As if it were that I had loved Bethan more, she would never have gone away.

I took it, and read it over, and she told me to take it away.

Dear Mum,

I don't know if you'll ever see this, but I needed to write this, to tell you, Mum. I am in a terrible place and I want to go home. If they find me they'll bind me to the Cables or make me join the Children of the Eye and I don't want to do that because then you're hollowed out and screaming forever, and the Queen on the TV has so many eyes and hands and everything is hot and dry and dying.

I'm scared, Mum. I wish I'd never left Swansea. I wish that I hadn't ever come here. Please Mum. Tell someone. Please. Please. I want to go home.

Bethan

Eight:

People troop into the entrance of the Brangwyn Hall, the fascia of which fills the frame; huge numbers of them, every one wearing some kind of robe; everyone androgynous, shaven headed, every one with an identically shaped bleeding wound, triangular, on the back of the scalp. In the extreme foreground, the wound on the nearest head can be seen in detail. There is something in there; something small and black, and it is hard to see but under the blood there could be an eye.

I woke up this morning, and I opened my bedroom curtains and looked out of the window, and saw the Guildhall. And then I closed my eyes. I closed my eyes and opened them, saw, for a second, the people from the picture, fresh blood on the backs of shaven heads, trooping silently into the gaping doors. I turned away and looked again, and they were still there. One of the people at the back began to turn, to look over a shoulder, and I looked away.

And I went into my kitchen and ate breakfast, and then I had a shower, went to the window again. The crowd had gone, and there was the Brangwyn Hall, doors shut.

Nine:

The inside of a house. You can see out of a bay window, see Brynmill Park outside. The floorboards are bare, no furniture here. Five people, men and women stand in ragged overalls, sideways on to the camera, bodies held in stiff, uncomfortable poses. Mouths open. Cables, electric cables entering the backs of their necks, falling to the ground and running out of shot. They could be screaming, twitching, writhing.

It was so obvious now, as if something had moved inside my head. There, ruined and empty and lost and never coming back. There she was. She'd been right.

I am more afraid now, I think, that I have been for a very long time. Not of old men in suits or thugs with diseased faces, or even of trees with limbs that writhe, or policemen who set you on fire, or wounds with eyes and fingers.

I'm most afraid of all now that I will lose myself and I will go looking for Bethan again. And that I will be out and I will see a turn I haven't been down before and I will walk down it and that no one will miss me when I have found her, and I do not come back.

The Austringer (1969)

When he lifts Mrs Mills' garage door and the rising light unveils the metal shelves, the boxes and the neat stacks of film cans, like a sheet being lifted, it is all Charlie can do not to utter the words, about bloody time.

"I can't tell you if there is anything of worth in here," says Mrs Mills. "It was Bernard's domain. He was really quite territorial about it." She is contained, made of short, straight lines. Straight back, straight hair, straight mouth. Even in her eighties, even though she might look on a photograph like she's made of straw, in person she has a gravity to her, a weight, like she's made of lead.

Charlie is intimidated by her, of course. "There isn't any way of knowing, Mrs Mills. Let me take a look. I'll let you know if I find anything worth keeping."

"I won't want to keep any of it." She is talking to the boxes.

"Um, well. If there's anything you could sell, then."

"Quite honestly, I wouldn't know." She takes a step back, seemingly without moving her feet. "I'll leave you to it?"

Charlie cannot fathom how anyone could not see what he sees here. These boxes, some stamped with BBC on the side, seem to him like fabulous treasures, thought lost; the faint smell of metal and must is like the puff of stale air that hit the face of Howard Carter as he cracked open Tutankhamun's tomb.

Can you see anything? Yes, wonderful things.

Five years, this took. Five years.

His breath is caught. Mrs Mills, beside him, is visibly pulling away, waiting with the barest minimum of politeness for the word. "Oh. Yes. Sorry. Yes. Of course. I'll come in later."

Even with Mrs Mills gone, Charlie restrains himself from running across the garage floor. He steadies himself on the metal upright of the shelf unit; it wobbles slightly, and he takes his weight off it. The cans are hefty things, designed to hold reels of 16mm film. He carefully lifts the top one from the stack in front of him, and although its label is perfectly visible, Charlie rubs the dust from it anyway, perhaps in case his eyes are deceiving him.

DR WHO." EPI. SIX

"POWER OF THE DALEKS"

•

You might know this: from the beginning of the 1960s through to the mid-70s, British TV shows were routinely thrown away. Things were different then: the idea of keeping a TV show on your shelf was no more feasible than bringing home a theatre production. With only two and eventually three channels, you either watched what was on the TV or you didn't, and if you missed a show, you missed it. Your favourite show was an appointment you kept or missed. Repeats didn't happen much.

They were recorded on two-inch videotape. And videotape was so expensive back then that after they'd made a copy on black-and-white film to sell abroad, this done by pointing a film camera at a flat TV screen, they'd tape over the programme with something else. *Dad's Army* with the snooker. *Doctor Who* with *Panorama*. Now of course, we see TV as a thing you can keep, and we expect to have everything in a commercially available box set, on our shelves or on demand, and the idea that television might be lost forever is alien to us. Enthusiasts have hunted down the film copies of missing television episodes for decades, travelling across the world, poring over the broadcast records of stations as far afield as Canada, Saudi Arabia, Nigeria, New Zealand. The things they bring back are only copies, often multiple generations down the line, things originally made in colour surviving in washed-out black-and-white echoes: the ghosts of television.

Occasionally you hear this rumour that a trove of this missing television might be found in the UK, in the hands of a private collector who for whatever reason — ignorance, selfishness, a need to own a thing that no one else has — has been sitting on it, keeping it hidden. Sensible enthusiasts consider these stories to be somewhere on a continuum between fondly held wishes and paranoid conspiracy theory. Father Christmas or Roswell, take your pick.

But, as Charlie picks through the contents of a suburban garage belonging to a retired television engineer, recently deceased, he begins to think that some of those rumours might have had some substance after all.

•

Charlie doesn't recognise everything; but when even Wikipedia has comprehensive lists of missing episodes of archive television and the 4G is decent, it only takes a few seconds to find what he suspects. Each can he lifts up has another treasure inside it. Something thought lost, something precious, sought after, unseen for decades.

The Power of the Daleks, parts one, two, three, five and six. Ten, fifteen, thirty more episodes of lost *Doctor Who*.

53

That one episode of *Doomwatch* that Charlie's father used to say was the best thing he'd ever seen on television, the one where Robert Powell's character dies failing to defuse a bomb. The BBC adaptation of a science fiction tale called *Immortality, Inc.* where a man who's about to die in a car crash winds up in a future where people can transplant their minds into other people's bodies. Two of the three missing episodes of *Dad's Army.* The episode of *Hancock's Half Hour* where Tony Hancock's been watching *Quatermass* and convinces himself that the unexploded bomb he finds in the back garden is an alien spaceship. A late night play, a ghost story called *The Austringer.*

Charlie is consciously moderating his breathing, trying not to hope. The film could be mouldy, cracked, decayed. The cans could be mislabelled, empty. The can — *The Austringer* — is flapping up and down in his hands, they're shaking so badly. He racks his brains, trying to think how he can get this to someone who had the kit and the know-how to restore it and still take the credit for finding it. Still get the money.

Five years, this took. Five years of buying a pint or four every Tuesday for the red-faced, pock-nosed old racist in the pub who seemed to know an awful lot about old telly and had an anecdote about everyone who ever worked at the BBC. Five years of angling to find out what he knew and what he'd really kept before the man got too drunk to make any sense. Five years of pretending to like the old bastard.

Until the night Mills had let Charlie walk him home, and Charlie had given him a cheery wave, and smiled, and thought, *God, I hope you die of a heart attack.*

And Bernard did, a couple of nights later. Only it was liver failure that got him.

Go to the funeral, and then leave it long enough to be sensitive, not long enough for her to clear things out.

Hello, Mrs Mills. We met at the funeral. Charlie, yes. That's right. I used to talk with Bernard at the pub. He asked me if I'd look after his old films and things. He thought they were worth something, but never got round to finding out, you see, and the last night I saw him, yes, at the pub, the last night I saw him, he asked me to come round and look over what he had and tell him if he could sell it. And I thought, well, I owed it to him to come and see.

Charlie steadies himself. Takes a deep breath. *He owes me this,* he thinks.

He puts the last can down, atop the fifth neat stack on the floor. He wavers about bothering to look in the boxes. They could be any old junk, anything. Nothing. Nothing to match the treasure in the cans, surely.

Charlie is imagining a season — no, a *year* of events in the BFI dedicated to his find, him on a seat at the front with the director and the head of the restoration team, being interviewed about the find in front of the audience. He is already rehearsing the story he's going to tell on stage, imagining the posture he'll adopt in his spotlit scene in front of the screen — he'll need a new suit. He'll need a haircut. He catches himself pushing his hair back.

"OK," he says to himself. He goes to a box, the one on the top, thick cardboard, metal edges and corners riveted on. He hefts it off the shelf and onto the concrete floor. It has a weight to it, but there is something hard inside, something that rattles. Kneeling, he works the lid off and it comes loose and off with a small, sudden *pumf* of released dust.

VHS cassettes. Full to the brim. Three boxes of them, the names on the tapes corresponding to the names on the film cans. He doesn't dare to hope, but why else would they be here? Bernard worked in TV. He had a line to people with the resources to — no. No. It can't be. Charlie pulls one out, looks at the label on the spine of it. *Hancock's Half Hour.*

A second one, *Doctor Who 4.* A third, *The Austringer.*

•

The Austringer was broadcast on Thursday, 18th December 1969 at 11.00pm, in colour, on BBC Two. Although its audience appreciation index was more than acceptable and the few notices it received were favourable (a critic in the *Evening Standard* called it, in passing, "a first-rate chiller" for instance), few people saw it, and the BBC only apparently made one black-and-white copy for sale overseas which, if the records are to be understood correctly, never got as far as being sold, perhaps out of a lack of confidence on the part of the BBC that viewers outside of the UK might even know what an austringer was.

•

Before he has even taken his coat off, Charlie, dust all down his front, is up in the attic looking for his old video machine, so overcome with excitement that he can barely get it back down the ladder without falling off and breaking his neck. He keeps telling himself that it's not true, it can't be, they're blank or they're mislabelled or they're episodes of Corrie, or the darts, or *The Bridge on the River Kwai* or *The Heroes of Telemark* something. I don't know, he tells himself, anything at all. But no matter the story he gives himself, he knows, *knows* that he's got a thing that's special.

These things have a pull to them. He can feel them tugging on him, a weird feeling. They want to be found. They want to be seen. This is it. This is the real thing.

He sets the video up under a small, spare Christmas tree that has no gifts beneath it, unplugs the fairy lights to make way for the video — Christmas is, after all, for quality television and film — and fumbles the connection, realises that he's looking at the wrong source, starts again, and gets it running. Then he sits down and puts in the video marked *Doctor Who 1*.

There it is. Wobbly, in the way that old videotapes are. The scene where Patrick Troughton looks in a mirror, and William Hartnell's face looks out at him. The distrust of Ben and Polly. The way the new Doctor refers to the Doctor in the third person, the conversation where he only replies with his eyebrows, tiny facial tics, and notes played on an old wooden recorder. The expression of subtle triumph on the Doctor's face when the Daleks recognise him. Not seen on any screen for fifty years, save Bernard Mills's.

Charlie begins, briefly, to cry.

The Horror Serial: He sees Tony Hancock, spooked by the last episode of *Quatermass and the Pit*, rushing back and forth through his house, his hysteria increasing, kinetic, infectious. The extreme close up of his face. "It's happened all over again... *Hancock and the Pit!*" The way the camera holds just long enough to be funny as the spooky music rises.

Survival Code: he sees the sweat on Tobias Wren's brow, under the pier, as he finds there's another wire on the bomb. The voice at the other end of the intercom, Dr Quist, says, "Don't pull it! Don't pull the wire! Follow it back to the terminal." Wren says, "I'm pulling the wire now." Back in the control room they breathe a sigh of relief. "You know, I think he's done it." That second of relief, and then the model shot of the pier, blown to pieces as the bomb goes up and Toby Wren with it.

He must have known, Charlie thinks. If he was just collecting old shows of interest he'd have episodes that were known to survive among the rarities. He'd have complete runs or partial runs of series. But everything Bernard Mills kept in his garage is a thing thought lost forever, junked, forgotten, the stuff of enthusiasts' and archivists' futile wishes. The vindictive old alcoholic knew what these things meant. He kept them for himself. He deprived the world of them. Charlie knows that he is better than that. He will make sure the world sees them. In a way that will ensure that everyone knows he found them.

He has to watch them all first, of course. To check they're all there. He has to. Of course he does.

He puts in the tape marked *The Austringer*. The picture, in black-and-white, of a bird's eye view, a lonely fen.

•

The camera settles on a car, a couple. They're quiet, she resting her hand on his knee. A thud; they stop the car, get out. A bird, dead. I think it's a hawk, says the man.

It's lying in the road, broken. It must have flown in front of us just as we were passing, says the man. *What's that?* says the woman.

She indicates a ring around its leg.

It must have belonged to someone, says the man. *Well, what do we do?* she says.

There's nothing we can do, the man replies.

They drive off. Atop the bluff, a tall, ragged figure stands in silhouette, unnoticed by the couple in the car. Beside him in white, the title: *The Austringer*

•

Charlie jolts awake. The low current buzz of the VCR, and his own breathing, the only sounds in the room. The screen lights the room up; the tape is paused. The jagged snowy lines criss-cross the screen, obliterate a face, gaunt, partly visible, staring out at him, its eyes gaping black pits in the snow, the only light in the room. It's — he looks at his phone, no notifications — about three in the morning.

He fumbles for the remote. He's sitting on it. He must have put his weight on it as he stirred and pressed pause. He's tired.

It's been a big day.

He presses stop and ejects the tape, as if apologising for abusing it. He brushes his teeth, but when he gets to his room lies down in his clothes and falls deeply asleep.

Charlie dreams of birds, of an old, gaunt man, tall and skinny and ragged, who sends the bird to hunt, watches it bring down a quail, and the camera of Charlie's dream, all in grainy black-and-white, travels back and forth, from bird to man to man to bird to man over and over, and those long gnarled arms swinging the lure, retrieving the kill, trudging to the summit of a bluff, looking out over a lonely, quite modern cottage.

Charlie feels a faint terror in the watching of this stiff and lonely figure, and a feeling that soon the bird will come for him, and conceives a desperate hope that the man's hooded eyes, like pits in shadow, will not turn towards him, nor that the picture in his dream will be frozen in video-pause snow for more than forty years.

59

A skinny, threadbare black-and-white figure, seen from behind, stoops over the broken body of the hawk. Long grey hair flutters in the wind, a battered wide-brimmed hat with feathers in its band, an old, long black coat, patched at the elbow. The owner of the hawk. Seen at this stage only in part, or in gaunt and ragged silhouette, he stands, looks out over a countryside as threadbare as he is.

We see battered shoes crossing a hillside serrated with terracettes and rocks, a shoulder across which that long, straight grey hair down flaps and whips. The movement of the man's hair is filmed to be faintly unsettling, faintly odd (an article Charlie read some years ago said something about how parts were filmed backwards, and sped up slightly to give a sense of wrongness).

The couple meanwhile pull up at the cottage they have rented for this weekend; as the play progresses we will find that their names are Greg and Leslie, that they are nervous and unwilling to have much to do with the outside world.

Greg calls a person we do not see, makes reference to the children, calls the unheard person at the other end "darling"; we are meant to infer that Greg and Leslie are conducting an affair, that they are lying to their respective spouses about where they are, who they are with.

The austringer — he isn't once called that in the play, of course, he only carries that name in the credits, for that is what he is, someone who hunts for game with a hawk, an austringer — is at the door of Greg and Leslie's cottage and in a tightly scripted scene that effectively marries tension and humour, he is asking for reparation, payment. It takes a while for Greg, an urban professional, to understand what the tall, sunken-cheeked man with the deep-set eyes and the long grey hair is getting at, and even then he still fails to understand really what the man wants. The man wants another trained hawk. There's half his meals and the money for the buying of the other half. There is a living, of sorts. Greg wouldn't know where to start; he insists on offering money, and the man says no, no, he wants a hawk, you see, a hawk like that one.

The conversation ends in frustration. A door slams. The old, tall man leaves empty-handed.

What a peculiar gentleman, says Greg to Leslie, and they agree. When they lie down together in bed that night, having forgotten about the hawk, the camera fixes in tight focus on two wedding rings left on the dressing table, the bodies beneath the sheet blurred in the background, beginning the languid movements of lovers.

•

Charlie takes an effort of no small will to shower and walk to the Tesco Extra to get some milk and something to eat for lunch; even as he's leaving the house he can feel the tapes pulling him back. He wants to see *The Highlanders, The Abominable Snowmen, The Faceless Ones;* he wants to be the lone disciple at the resurrection of these lost artefacts, who will then spread the good news of their resurrection from televisual death.

They are alive, they are alive.

Once he's eaten his lunch — a sandwich, hastily scoffed on the way home — he can't take any more, he has to see. He drops the sandwich wrapper in the hall and all but runs for the lounge, as if scared that his hoard will vanish.

He closes the curtains and picks up *The Austringer.* But he thinks, maybe something else, so he settles down with five episodes in a row of *Adam Adamant Lives!* They're not great TV; Gerald Harper, in the title role, is too arch, too knowing, the direction too pedestrian, the plots too slow. But that isn't the point, because there are men like Charlie who would sell their own children to have them, even on old VHS tapes.

The Loneliness of the Long Distance Walker. Charlie sees Captain Mainwaring call Pike "you stupid boy," and that's nothing special, Arthur Lowe delivered the line dozens of times in dozens of episodes, but no one has seen him deliver it in *this* episode, no one has seen Clive Dunn tell everyone not to panic in *this* script for nearly five decades. It is a delight.

It's late again. Time for the ghost story. Charlie replaces *The Austringer* in the machine, and tries to rewind to a place he remembers seeing, but he ends up so close to the start that he decides he might as well watch the whole thing again.

•

In grainy black-and-white — Charlie thinks forward to how beautiful this will look when restored for DVD — the lovers are eating; they talk. They're very middle class, plummy, talking the talk of theatre shows and office colleagues and city life, of mutual friends who do not know the truth about them. But never quite of spouses, never of children. The conversation slides past these things, skirts around the central truths of their lives. Greg and Leslie are not likeable people. But they're human.

The noise of smashing glass outside interrupts Leslie mid-sentence, brings Greg to his feet. Outside; the passenger's side window of the car has been broken; a hand reaches into the ashtray, takes out some cigarette butts, some ash. Greg gets outside in time to see someone dash behind a tree. The austringer is gone. Greg checks the car to see if anything has been stolen, can't find anything.

The scene changes. Now the old man is alone in his small, spare home, so different to the lovers'. The incidental music, a gentle melody played on a single flute, rises a little, haunts you. The camera focusses tightly onto his hands as he works the butts and ash into a lump of wax, and the wax into two wax dolls. He puts them next to the fire. Then the old, gnarled hand holds the foot of a bird. And throws it into the fire.

He mumbles something. The music stops, abruptly. Three knocks at the door, three at the window.

The austringer looks up. Two faces, the faces of women, aquiline, birdlike, hair falling over eyes that are in shadow or entirely absent, long-fingered hands pressed against the glass.

Back in their cottage, Greg and Leslie sit on the bed, across from each other. The incidental music, the flute, begins to trill and both of them look up, expressions of sudden dread etched on handsome faces unaccustomed to fear. The flute sounds merge into the sound of screeching in the night outside.

The sound of feathered wings beating against glass.

•

Again, Charlie has drifted off to sleep; again, he jolts awake.

The screen is paused again, the snow over the eyeless face in the window. He decides to press play, try to make sense of it regardless.

•

Greg, in a dressing gown, is in the cottage kitchen. He's making tea. A rattle of the window makes him jump, and he throws tea all over himself. He groans, gets a teatowel, dabs at himself. A face, eyes in shadow, appears in the window behind him, briefly, just enough to make you wonder what you saw in an age before pause and rewind.

The door of the kitchen slams shut. *Leslie?* he says. He tries the door. It won't open. He starts to call for Leslie with more urgency, more volume.

Leslie sits at the dressing table. She unties her hair, looks down for the brush, looks up and sees the reflection of those two birdlike women with feathers in their matted hair, eyes obscured with pits of blackness, in long white May-Queen dresses of an earlier age. One raises a hand, reaching towards her. She spins around, and no one is there. She takes deep, juddering breaths. Calms herself down.

Then a long-nailed hand falls on her shoulder. She screams now, falls off the stool, scrambles for the door, almost on her hands and knees.

The kitchen door flies open. Greg hears the screams of rushes to the stairs, his hand on the bannister as Leslie falls headlong, screaming, then silent.

She lands in a heap at the bottom. There is a sickly crack. Her face is staring, open-mouthed, open-eyed.

•

Charlie doesn't know why he keeps falling asleep.

The ringing of the phone wakes him. It's Mrs Mills.

"I hadn't heard anything from you," she says, without any apology for calling late — is it late? Charlie isn't sure — "I wondered if you had any idea of the value."

"Ah. Right. Yeah, yeah. Right. I can't be sure," he says. "I have had a look at the cans and I've not found anything of value yet. I can't even be sure that what's written on the cans is what's on the film, to be honest."

"Do the labels suggest the film is valuable?"

It begins to dawn on Charlie that she might have had a better idea of the value of the cache in the garage than she might have let on.

"I, well, I don't know for sure —"

"What about the tapes? Aren't they recorded with the contents of the cans?"

She knows, he thinks.

"I — maybe. I, uh, I don't have a video any more." He is apologetic, but silently willing her to get off the line.

A pair of pale, black-eyed faces stare out of the screen at him from behind snow. He turns to look the other way, at the wall.

"I was not expecting you to take them all away with you if you had no means of watching them," she says.

"Yeah. I — I'm going to see a mate about them tomorrow."

"You'll keep me updated?" She is sharp, persistent.

"Yes. I certainly will. Thank you, Mrs Mills."

She hangs up. How to do this without her knowing?

He ignores the phone the next time it rings, and the next, and then the battery dies and it is silent. And then he sleeps right there in the armchair. It's dark when he wakes up. He's hungry, thirsty. But there is more TV to watch. It matters. He gets up and puts in *The Abominable Snowmen* and watches, rapt, doesn't notice when he pisses himself.

There's only him in this room, with the TV and a pile of tapes with magic on them. They need to be watched.

He decides to watch *The Austringer* again.

Something smashes outside. There is a rustling sound behind Charlie and then the never-used lock on the lounge door goes *click*, all by itself. Charlie doesn't move. He has television to watch. Lost television, unearthed, in black-and-white copy; the ghost of television.

•

Greg runs out of the house, holding a fire poker. And there is the austringer, walking away over the hill. He runs after the man. Whose pace doesn't slow or speed up.

A fractured cat and mouse game ensues, but as soon as the city man thinks he might catch the warlock, he is gone, only to reappear on another hill, in another direction. Everything is jagged, the camera angles skewed, the cuts swift and disorienting. And then Greg isn't the hunter. Here are those two eyeless figures. They approach him, come rushing towards him through the trees. Greg runs headlong over the moor, crouches behind a rock, eyes screwed shut. You know they're just above the rock, a woman's hand rests on it just above the top of Greg's head, a pale, dirty hand with long fingers and long nails. Greg's nerve breaks, and he gets up and runs, and it's all close-ups of his face. Then it's a wider shot, and Greg arrives in a cairn, a circle of stones.

A shot from a high angle. Terrified, Greg clings to the stone in the middle of the circle. Two figures in white, hair matted, advance on him at four and eight o'clock. He stands up, backs away. Behind him, at the twelve o'clock point, a third figure enters the circle. Leslie, pale and her eyes in shadow, still in her nightgown, reaching for him.

66

•

Charlie stares, transfixed at the screen. The picture quality is worse than ever, and adjusting the tracking seems to do nothing, but it is as if the pagan apparition of Leslie's ghost is here in the room standing in front of him, eyeless. He can feel black-and-white wind on his skin, drizzle in his hair.

The quality of the picture is deteriorating. He can't find the remote. He is there now, standing next to Greg, the phantoms coming closer. And the gaunt warlock, still bereaved of his hunting bird, at the edge of the circle looking in. But the picture grows fuzzier, as the old man, expressionless, turns and walks away into video-distorted darkness.

Everything is doused with snow.

Charlie can't hear what Greg is trying to say; but the camera is in tight close up on him and there isn't a Greg there any more, just Charlie in his place and none of this makes sense, neither the ending of the play nor the ending of his evening makes any sense to him at all; he hammers with the heels of his hands against the inside of the screen, and then everything crashes into blackness.

•

A week later Cora Mills, claiming to be convinced that Charlie has absconded with her late husband's treasures, will call the police on Charlie. They will break into his house, but they shall not find him, only an armchair that smells of urine, a television still on, showing nothing, a stack of empty film cans and three neat piles of videotapes, all blank.

67

Leave

1

Things have always been this way, says Ana, scratching at her hairline with short, chipped blue fingernails. Her roots are showing, brown beneath shocking pink. *We woke up and things were the way they always had been, and if we thought different, we were only dreaming.*

The bus changes gear, and it turns onto the road that runs across the river. The Great Ziggurat gleams in the sun, its polished black stones dazzling May. She taps on her sunglasses and they slip down off her forehead over her eyes. She licks her lips, folds her arms, wraps her right hand around the left side of her ribcage.

— *You can't say that,* she says. It's too close to what she knows. It frightens her. She looks across the bus, through the opposite window, past a man with heavy grey stubble. The man looks at her, and May turns back to Ana. I *mean— you just— it's not the time. The place.*

Ana looks as if she's going to say something. She doesn't. The bus stops. The man with the heavy grey stubble gets off and an old woman in a blue overcoat that smells of sour milk gets on, takes the man's place. May doesn't know her, doesn't look at her. She knows the woman is watching her. The people they send are always like this: decrepit, foul-smelling, aged. She keeps her silence for the half-hour, until.

— *I think this is our stop.*

Ana leans across May, her arm brushing her chest, pushes the button.

2

May tries not to look at the Herms and the Paniscae that frolic around them; they scare her.

She strides past, and soon they are out of sight behind the first of the blocks. She wishes she had a coat or a jacket or a scarf or something, feeling exposed in just a T-shirt, wondering how many of the cracked windows of the estate have behind them pairs of ancient, watery eyes assigned to watch her, gnarled liver-spotted hands on curtains, hairy mouths chewing on toothless gums.

Ana doesn't seem to notice May's discomfort. She says, too loudly,

— *God, what a dump.*

The sentence echoes across the cracked concrete and asphalt between the flats, and the wind gusts, briefly, as if on cue; ruffling leaves that lie in the gutter across the way between cigarette ends and used condoms. There isn't a tree for miles.

The back of May's head prickles again. The sun withdraws behind a cloud.

3

The building is smaller than the others, but still, like all the buildings here, the product of nineteen-sixties brutalism, all concrete panels and cracked glass. It catches the shadow of the tower block above it, and the odd light makes it look discoloured, uneven, rickety, as if it were about to fall at any moment.

The door is patched with plywood, a cracked wired pane of glass taking up most of its upper half. May can't see inside. The two women stand in front of it for a moment.

— *Are you going to ring or what?* says Ana.

May presses the doorbell. A low buzz comes from inside. After a while, a man opens the door. He must be in his early twenties, dressed in grubby jeans and T-shirt. His dark hair is long and falls over a long face, half-covering round bottle-bottom glasses. May steps forward; squinting, the man retreats a step.

— *David Bateson?* she says.

He lifts a slender hand, brushes back a lock of hair that immediately falls back into place.

— *Peter. David's upstairs.*

— *Ah. I'm May. May Simon. We, ah spoke on the phone. I spoke with David. About some help you can give me.*

— *The magician.*

— *I don't know what you're talking about.*

Ana is looking at her quizzically.

It's difficult for May to tell what Peter Bateson's eyes are doing behind those glasses. His face makes a sort of please yourself expression, and then subsides into that curious blankness.

— *Oh right. Come in, then.*

— *We own the whole place,* he explains. *But we only live in the west wing. There's only the three of us.*

It's less a home, more some kind of open-plan multi-storey garage, as vast and rickety and grey inside as it is outside. The door opens onto a flat expanse of concrete, covered with boxes and sundry electrical items, fridges, freezers, washing machines, televisions with their backs hanging off, videos with the pop-up cradle for the tape open, with something moving inside.

Peter negotiates an awkward, winding path around the obsolete devices, to a ladder, and up to the edge of the half-collapsed upstairs floor.

— *Careful,* he says.

The upstairs is much like downstairs, but the goods are smaller. A Bush radio sits on a coil of wire. Three portable CRT TVs sit, one on top of another. There a stack of microwave ovens; there a heap of desk lamps; there a half-dozen beige PC towers arranged as if in conclave. In the corner of the floor there's a flat, with a frosted, reinforced glass door. The light filters in through high, grubby windows, partially obscured by hanging cables, stacks of boxes.

The flat is cramped and noisy, the brown once-patterned carpet strewn with tools and electronic parts; the shelves full of radios and TVs, Playstations and ZX Spectrums and Sega Megadrives and 1980s boomboxes. Peter leads them into a sort of living room, clears away a couple of heaps of circuit boards and solder reels from the sofa, encourages them to sit down.

In the middle of the floor, a young man who looks exactly like Peter sits with his back to them, tapping on a controller attached to an old console, directing the movements of a pixelated woman in a skintight catsuit on a flickering, snowy cathode-ray television as she leaps and somersaults across platforms, shooting aliens and picking up glowing crystals.

May motions towards him.

— *Is that—?*

— *That's Jonathan. David will be out in a moment.*

Ana throws herself down on the sofa, and something under the seat cushion goes plink, a glassy little sound; the sofa cushion doesn't really bounce back up under her.

— *Oops,* she says.

She leans forward, towards Jonathan, who hasn't removed his attention from the TV.

— *Hey. Hey. Hey. What you playing?*

— *Bayonetta.* He doesn't look away.

There's an explosion on screen, as something big and tentacled and green spits a ball of fire tries at the catsuit-clad woman with the swirling ponytail, who leaps back and forth and up and down in time with the man's fingers, shooting steadily at the thing until it explodes with a satisfying pop. Words fly towards the front of the screen in big silver letters and the repetitive music changes in key.

May and Ana both watch over his shoulder. It's hypnotic. May loses track of how long she's been here.

5

A man comes out. He looks almost exactly like Peter, only he's in a grubby blue T-shirt with a cracked Nike swoosh on it.

— *Oh, hey. What have you got for me?* he says.

May stands up and drops her bag from her shoulder, opens it, takes out an object the size of a small paperback book, a small box made of plastic in black and discoloured white. Hands it to him.

Ana looks over her shoulder.

— *What—?*

David pushes back his thick dark hair the same way that his brother does. He turns the thing over in his hands, draws breath gently through his teeth, lets it out in a sigh.

— *Stereo Eight. Nice. You know what this—?*

— *Yeah. Can you play it?* says May.

He pushes his tongue into his cheek, runs it around his lower lip, nods.

— *Do you know what's on it?*

May half-shakes her head, scratches the back of her scalp, feels a little irregularity under her hair.

— *Not really.*

David clears a pile of old Sinclairs and Commodores from the scratched formica dining table, and they sit around it. He hooks up some wire with crocodile clips to a transformer, and then to what looks like an old car radio with a slot the same size as the plastic box. He leaves the room for a second, and comes back in with a couple of speakers, which he connects to the radio with bits of tape and two pairs of spring-loaded pincers. Then he inserts the cartridge into the player.

There's a judder, the sound of something whirring, and then over the sound of crackly, far-away cheering crowds, a woman with the kind of refined, precise voice that no one has used since before May and Ana were born, says:

— *Here, inside the inner courtyard, is a world in waiting, a little pool of silence in a world of sound. Her Majesty is already in her fairytale golden coach, drawn up under the portico of the grand entrance, and any second now in all her splendour, and gold... and scarlet of her postilion, she will drive away from her home into the world waiting outside. And now, the coach moves. The coach is leaving the Queen's home, on the greatest day of her life...*

The recording fades out.

Ana says,

— *I don't understand. What Queen? That's not the Queen. What is this?*

May smiles a brief, sad smile.

— *This is what you were talking about. On the bus.*

— *I don't understand.*

David is staring at May, intently, through those thick glasses, unreadable. The recording fades back in. More cheering; a man this time, again with that thick, affected accent.

— *And in Trafalgar Square, the excitement of the vast throngs of people rises to its first great climax of the day, because the leading units of Her Majesty's procession are already threading through the central arc of the Admiralty Arch, under the great Royal Cipher in gold on a crimson field and flanked by two huge gilt anchors, heavily decorated with*

74

knotted golden ropes. Now comes the climax, the glittering living necklace of pomp winds past; now we await the richest jewel of all: the golden coach, Her Majesty, His Royal Highness, coming now under the Admiralty Arch, coming into the square, and the crowd receives them as only a British crowd in London could...

And it's gone again. And there's no more on the cartridge. David gets up.

— *I think you should leave now,* he says. *There's a back way.*

He leads them out of the flat, up another two flights of stairs and out a door at the end of what seems like a half-mile of corridor. Although they went up three floors, although grubby sunlight has been filtered through all the windows they've passed on the lower floors, May and Ana find themselves on an outside path, laid in gravel, fringed with grass. One side of the path is bordered by a high wall. On the other side, the grass disappears into an opaque white mist, as does the path ahead.

Behind them, David Bateson says,

— *Don't come back. Please.*

He shuts the door, and they hear it lock. The path stretches ahead.

6

Ana kicks at a stone. It hurtles off the path and into the mist; it abruptly ceases to make a sound.

— *I hate it when this happens,* she says.

May puts a hand against the wall.

— *Here,* she says, *Give me a step up, will you?*

75

Ana clasps her hands, crouches; may steps on them, reaches and grabs the top of the wall with both hands, heaves herself up for a second, looks over, bounces back down again.

— *So?* says Ana.

— *Long way down. A really long way. Miles.*

Ana nods.

— *What about the other way?*

May bites her lip, rests one hand on the top of her head, hooks the other in one of the pockets in her jeans. She blows through her teeth.

— *Best to stick to the path, I think. Look.*

She motions back along the path with a casual gesture. it goes on, forever. forward and back, vanishing into the mist.

— *Fuck's sake,* says Ana.

May shrugs.

— *These things happen.* She starts walking. *Come on, then. No point whinging.*

Ana scuffs her feet on the path.

— *You gonna tell me what that tape was about, then?*

May sighs.

— *You know what you were talking about on the bus?*

— *Um?*

Ana shrugs. May begins anyway.

— *Some people think that maybe the Great Black Ziggurat of Old London Town was not always there, or rather that it wasn't always always there. If you catch my drift.*

— *Not really. Go on, anyway.*

— *The story goes that there was supposed to be a great house there, or maybe two houses. And a clock. A massive clock, which had a man's name.*

— *A name? What sort of a name?*

— *Jack. Ben. Tom. Something like that. Something old and informal.*

— *That's silly.*

— *There's other things. Buckingham Palace was supposed to be made of white stone, rather than brass, and that the Queen was different, that she was a real person, just an old lady with white hair and with only the one body. She was old. She got old. Like a normal person. She'd been there sixty years maybe, and there were others before her. And there weren't any Herms or Paniscae. And Stonehenge was a clapped-out ruin. And the policemen kept their faces. Things were different.*

She licks her lips, and continues.

— *You have to imagine, for the sake of argument, that at some point, someone decided that the world would be a better place, or a more interesting place, if it changed, not just in the present, but in the past as well, and that they figured out how. It's a theory. You don't have to believe it. But anyway, the point is that because it was done by someone, because someone made it, it's not perfect. You know how when you tape over something on the video and you get little random bits of old TV at the beginning of the tape, no matter how much you rewound the tape before you hit record? It's like that. There was something before, and even though most things have been all taped over, tiny bits and pieces get left behind.*

— *So this tape of yours,* says Ana.

— *Yeah.*

77

— *You think it's-?* She cocks her head to one side, as if motioning towards some possibility.

— *Yeah.*

— *Where did you-?*

— *We found it in— I mean when we went through his. He had it.*

— *Oh.* Ana looks away. They walk some distance in the mist before she speaks again. *So what are you going to do with it?*

— *I'm going to keep it very safe.* May stops, wheels around, bars Ana's way. *You can't tell anyone. Promise.*

— *Yes. Absolutely,* says Ana, *hand in hair. Yeah. No question.*

May composes herself, looks a little embarrassed. She turns back to the path and starts walking without any further word. They walk silently through the mist for another few minutes.

— *I think we might be getting to the end,* says May. She points. Indistinct, something resembling a building appears, not far ahead.

— *May,* says Ana.

— *Mm?*

May doesn't turn around.

— *Your tape. Is it important?*

— *No. No, I don't think so.*

The path ends, abruptly, as if interrupted mid-flow by a building that appears at its end, a concrete box identical to the one they left, only taller, stretching a dozen floors up, and more dilapidated still. The glass in the plywood door has, at some time in the past, been smashed; someone covered the hole, clumsily, with two panels from a cardboard box and a few strips of gaffer tape. The board hangs off now, the cardboard sodden and mouldy, the shards of wired glass still remaining in the ruined window visible, the ends of wire rusty, the edges of the glass dull.

Inside, it's dark. Ten feet away, and May can smell the decay, the mould and the damp and the rot.

They pause at the door. May looks up, imagines, just for a second, that a tattered half-hanging curtain in a window one floor up twitches; she gets a glimpse of a shaking, liver-spotted hand withdrawing into the dark. No, it was a large moth or something. No, it was a rat. No, she imagined it.

— *I don't like it,* May says.

Ana shrugs.

— *It's the exit, innit?* she says.

Ana pushes the door open with the tips of her fingers.

7

Inside, the stink is even worse, like books left in a leaky garage for ten years or more. The carpet, so filthy and blackened that its pattern has changed into something threatening and shadowy, gives lightly under their feet, but doesn't spring back, and as May looks down, a shoal of silverfish scoot away from her left foot. Artex on the walls carries streaks and markings that in the all-but absent light give the impression that it moves under its own power.

Ana calls out.

— *Hello? Anyone here?*

May flaps her hands.

— *No! No, don't!* She sounds too high-pitched. Her breathing is faster than it should be. She lowers her voice an octave.

— *Let's just find a way out onto the street.*

A rat. A cobweb. A bird nesting in the hole left by a dangling light fitting and a smashed-up polystyrene ceiling tile; it flaps around in Ana's face and she screams and bats it away and May has to grab her arm to stop her belting into the depths of the building.

By the time they make it to the ground floor front of the building, May and Ana are ready to run; they collide with the front door, find it chained and padlocked from the outside. May grabs a broken chair from the lobby floor and swings it against the glass in the door, twice. The first time, it bounces off; the second time, the glass disintegrates, like a downward wave.

Ana takes off her jacket and puts it across the window frame, and May helps her climb through. As May clambers through the hole behind her, she hears a rumbling, like the sound of a dozen pairs of feet running down the building's stairs.

May falls in a heap on the marble step outside the door, puts her hand in something slimy on the ground. The thundering stops abruptly. No one appears.

May realises that she is very cold. Ana's at the bottom of the steps on the pavement. She's looking down the street.

— *I think I know where we are,* she says.

May looks at her hand. Birdshit. Walking down to the pavement, she fumbles in her jacket pocket, finds a tissue, wipes her hand, crumples the tissue, throws it into the gutter among the cigarette ends and the crisp packets.

She looks back at the building, one of three that face a courtyard, all near-derelict. The fragments of sign above the foyer read:

G IMS ADE H SE

— *We'd better get going,* says Ana.

She nods towards the corner of the courtyard. A policeman and a policewoman have just turned the corner. They stop, and the empty dark spaces beneath their headgear where their faces should be turn towards the two women. May and Ana leave, walking quickly, not looking.

May hears something laugh, something old and muffled and in the building behind them.

It turns out that the building is two corners away from the Bateson brothers' home, and one more from the square with the Herms and Paniscae, and the bus stop.

The two police officers follow May and Ana for a short while, and then abruptly turn away. As they go, May turns around and catches, in the corner of her eye, a curtain swishing shut in a second-floor window.

At the bus stop, they stand in the gathering mist. It's already getting dark. The bus arrives, and they get on and Ana hands their tickets to the driver, who does a double-take, stares at them as if appalled by something, and hands them back without a word.

The only other passenger is a wrinkled, dusty man with only a few misbehaving wisps of white hair, who chews on his gums and stares, even when May meets his eye. She looks away, aware of the eyes fixed on the nape of her neck. Ana says,

— *Here.*

She shows May the tickets. The destination now reads:

When the bus arrive at their stop, Ana hands the tickets to May. She looks at them, as if wondering what to do, and then crumples them, puts them in the ticket bin at the front of the bus.

— *What now?* says Ana as they disembark, the old man still staring.

— *Tonight's still on. I'll go home and change.*

Ana nods.

— *Ryan coming?*

— *Oh, I expect so.*

— *OK. Drop you a text.*

The friends part, and May walks home under orange streetlights that dye the wintery mist with a warm, fiery colour, that only makes it feel colder. Her feet ache.

For May, this kind of thing has always been the way, as long as she can remember; the more magic you know, the more things you find. The more things you find, the more they watch you, and the more they watch you, the more you feel the need to run away, the more temptation there is to go join the Paniscae, or to turn up at the doors of the Changing Room and let them change you into something that isn't afraid any more.

You can't live with fear; in the end, all there is for May is to ignore it, and to go on living.

And that means the occasional night out, no matter whether she feels like it or not.

8

Ten o'clock: Ryan Hood and Ana Jones and May in the pub that sits in the shadow of the British Museum, engulfed by that thousand-foot-high structure of brass and black basalt, the repository of all history, the sign that the Queen of England, whose Name must never be spoken, holds sway over the past as well as the future.

Ryan has brought someone that May doesn't know, a young woman with a translucent heart-shaped face, dressed in a short black coat and heavy knee-high boots. Ryan introduces her to May, and May nods and smiles and flicks a lock of hair out of her eyes and says hello, and neglects to say that she has failed to catch the newcomer's name.

Still, the mild social quandary raised by this fact no more than adds to the discomfort that May already feels at the stranger's presence.

She's watching May. Sure, Ryan's friend is sitting there between May and Ryan and making conversation, and sure, every time May looks, the girl is not looking at her, but May knows. Those wide green eyes are watching May closely. She's used to being watched. She knows.

And how does this person know Ryan? She doesn't fit. She looks young in a way that Ana doesn't, with a studded strap around her neck and the kind of short, shining asymmetrical black hair that takes hours in a stylist and rings in her ears and eyeliner that flips up just so, and defined, heavy eyebrows and well-drawn lips and a ring in her nose and a ring in the middle of her lower lip that distorts it slightly, giving an impression of sweet, smiling serenity, of a kind of innocence.

She doesn't fit here. And she is watching May. But not in the way the people behind the curtains watch May.

In the way that May is watching her.

Come chucking out time, Ryan and Ana have already agreed to go to a club; of course, it was the plan all along. May had thought they were both looking well-turned out. May has long suspected that something was going on between the two of them, and it surprises her when they beg her to go with them.

She says, yeah, sure. She doesn't want to be alone tonight.

They walk out into the shadow of the Basalt Museum, on the pavement, bathed in the orange light of a lamp post, surrounded by migrating punters. Ryan's friend stands herself directly in front of May and says, to her, not Ryan:

— *Mind if I tag along? I'm at a bit of a loose end.* She smiles, and tucks her shining hair behind one ear with a long, perfect fingernail, a liquid, glossy black.

May turns and looks at Ryan. He shrugs with his face.

— *Sure,* he says.

Ana is silent. She is staring at the woman, who is staring at May.

On the way to the club, May walks sandwiched between Ana on her left and the dark-haired woman on her right, each intent on holding a conversation with her while excluding the other.

Ryan, above all this, walks a few paces behind. Ana tries to bring in in-jokes and references to people May's new friend cannot possibly know; the other tries to make the conversation wholly about May.

The effect induces a kind of claustrophobia in May. She wants to tell them both not to be so silly, that they are grown women, that they remind her of schoolgirls jockeying for the attention of the popular girl, but she loves Ana too much not to notice something is very wrong; she does not know the dark-haired woman enough to be so rude.

The newcomer's soft, cold hand brushes against May's. May glances down at her, meets her eye, feels a little dizzy for a moment.

They find somewhere where the dress code will accommodate May's jeans without any trouble at all.

The place plays the kind of techno that people outside of London listen to. Tribes of twentysomethings mingle, without mixing. It's as hot here as it is cold outside, oppressively so, and May does a bad thing, a thing she really shouldn't: caressing the half-inch of rough-cut copper pipe on the thong around her neck, she focusses her inner eye on the word YOUTH, and, eyes closed, rearranges the letters to make a sigil. The symbol now she makes her all, her everything, a new letter in an alphabet of desire. The movements of her dance become repetitive, a ritual.

An aura of clean, fresh, cool air gathers around May. It does strange things to the ultraviolet light, and May's skin gleams. She catches sight of herself in the mirror behind the bar. She looks youthful, and invincible, and not at all thirty-five, and not at all tired. She approves.

May knows that eyes will see, that consequences will accrue, but she doesn't care.

Tonight, she wants the illusion of power.

She wants to be free.

May leaves Ryan to go buy drinks for the others, declined the offer of her own drink with a wave and a smile, striding to the dance floor.

The beat is cleansing; she closes her eyes and gives herself up. She moves. Everything is in the release. Partly, it's her spell, keeping her cool and fresh and comfortable, but partly it's just the music, her need to forget her fear and her grief (and they're really the same feeling, aren't they?)

She dances alone in the crowd, blissed out. The warmth of the bodies around her shifts; another body begins to dance close to hers, hands almost touch her. She opens her eyes, and meets those dark eyes, fixed steadily upon her; the spark of recognition comes, too late. A strange feeling of transgression causes her diaphragm to contract.

But May is a magician. She forges the world with her will. Everything she does is transgression.

She goes with it.

The trance breaks. May needs some water. She leaves the dancefloor, taking the dark-haired woman by the hand as if it's the most natural thing, as if they're best friends.

She buys two bottles, empties her own in two draughts. May leaves the woman by the bar and looks around for Ryan and Ana. The woman appears at her shoulder.

— *Where'd they go?*

— *Dunno,* says May. I'll text.

She pulls out her phone. One new message. She hadn't felt it go off. It's from Ryan.

— *ana not well taking her home*

May checks the time. Ryan sent her the text an hour ago. She'd been on the floor for a whole hour before that.

86

Suddenly, she feels very tired. The spell wears off a little. Her arms and back ache, and her feet throb. She turns to the dark-haired woman.

— *I'm off home,* she says.

Ryan's friend nods.

— *Where do you live?*

— *Acton.*

The woman leans over and takes May's hand.

— *Tell you what. I'll split a cab with you.*

9

Standing next to the coat check, waiting for Ryan's friend to get her coat, May orders a cab, and now they're out and waiting. A few people are leaving the club, the trickle before the flood, not enough for them to have to stand too close together, and yet May's companion is standing close enough for the skin on May's arm to tingle slightly with the proximity.

May tries to distract herself, falls into the old ritual of scanning windows, roofs, the corners of alleyways, looking for the tips of palsied fingers, for the reflection of rheumy eyes.

— *There's no one watching,* she says out loud.

The dark-haired woman raises an eyebrow.

— *Should there be?* she says.

— *No,* says May.

The dark-haired woman turns, carelessly, brushes her fingers across the back of May's hand, which is the sort of gesture that could be an accident, if May wants it to be.

In the cab, May asks how the dark-haired woman knows Ryan (they met at work, apparently, although May cannot parse the chronology or circumstance of that meeting in any meaningful way). The conversation dries up. The stranger looks across at May with her hands folded in her lap, her lips pressed together in a small smile. The streetlights glint off the ring in her nose, the ring in her lip, on and off. May tries not to maintain eye contact. The dark-haired woman looks out of the window. — *Haven't we passed here?* she says.

The girl points — they are passing the building where the Batesons live and its courtyard full of Herms.

May shudders as she always does when she passes by here, as she did five minutes ago, when they passed by here last time.

— *Aw, no,* says May. *Not again.*

The dark-haired girl leans across May and taps on the glass partition.

May, sitting with her back to the driver, turns around sees in the corner of her eye the driver half-crumble, half-dissolve into a cloud of dust or mist that dissipates to nothing. The cab slowly comes to a halt.

— *Well,* says May's companion. *At least we don't have to pay.*

May glances at the woman, and then she turns around and kneels on her seat, opens the communication hatch and checks the meter: it has stopped. She digs in her purse and pulls out three ten-pound notes, making a conscious effort not to look at the picture of the Queen on the front, as you must. She drops them through the window onto the front seat.

The light that shows the doors are locked turns off.

— *Better start walking,* says May.

May finds herself, as she steps out of the cab, staring into the empty eyes of the Herms: limbless, priapic, blank, bolted to their posts, like the ones she read about once that they had in Ancient Greece, only the ones in Greece were made of stone, not people. She gets that cold feeling in the pit of her gut that she always gets and thinks about what it must be like — and then thinks that no, she must not.

— *That way,* she says, pointing towards the waste ground.

— *Do you know where we are?* says the girl, as they pick their way across stony, scrubby ground.

— *Kind of. Don't worry.* May avoids eye contact.

— *What are you scared of? What's wrong?*

— *Nothing.*

May stands there for a moment, wondering how she's going to get out of this place alive.

— *Oh, sod it,* she says at length.

May takes off the little ring of copper and brass that hangs around her neck, and letting the thong dangle, she holds it up between between thumb and forefinger. She blows through it, and closes her eyes. She imagines, engraved behind her eyelids, the sigil for HOME, and forgets herself, becoming only the focus for the sigil. She lets the metal drop, catching it by the thong and letting it swing. She stretches out her arm and holds it out one way, and then another, until the ring gives out a sound — and she is never sure if it is audible objectively or in her imagination — not unlike the ringing of a half-full wineglass with a wet finger running around the rim.

By the time that they have travelled a hundred yards along the street, every building has become a featureless cube of black stone, separated from the street and its neighbours by short stretches of rubble-strewn wasteland. May points across a stretch of flat, soiled ground.

— *We'll be fine if we head this way.*

Ryan's friend has her hands folded, almost primly. She looks up at the taller woman, clicks at the ring in her lip with her teeth. *You sure?*

— *No,* says May. *Better be quick, though. I don't want to stay here.*

The fluttering in May's gut returns; it dawns on her that her new friend has made no comment on what she has done. She follows May quietly, and looks at her in that strange way when she thinks May is not looking at her.

Magic in a place like this has its risks.

They pick their way across stones and hunks of broken concrete, blackened kitchenware, rotting magazines, broken powertools, and abandoned, filthy toys. The dark-haired woman's boots, all platforms, straps and heels, aren't designed for walking in a place like this, and May frequently has to stretch out a hand to steady her companion.

After a while, they are holding hands and not letting go.

A light becomes visible a few hundred yards away, flickering, and sometimes obscured by moving shapes in the dark.

— *I think it's a campfire,* says May.

— *Oh,* says the dark-haired woman. *Is this safe?*

— *I think this is good. I think we're going to be all right.*

Twenty yards or so from the perimeter of the firelight, they stop and hide behind two upturned, skeletal fridge-freezers. May squeezes the woman's hand and lets go, looks more closely at the camp around a rusty white corner.

She sees about ten men and women. They are giants, the smallest of them seven, eight feet tall. Each has shining, faintly iridescent bluish-black skin, a wide, generous mouth, obliquely angled black eyes with pupils so wide they have no whites. They are naked but for strings of dyed seashells, pale leather straps for knives and quivers of arrows, their sexualities potent, present. Full breasts, rings in nipples, vaginas and cocks, pubic hair shaved and braided and dyed, like the rest of the hair on the giants' bodies.

May turns and smiles, finds herself an inch away from the face of the dark-haired woman, who was looking out over her shoulder. The woman's lips part slightly. May pauses a moment, looks into the her eyes. She turns her head.

— *Sorry,* says May's companion.

May wriggles away, catches her breath.

— *It's OK. It's all going to be OK,* she says.

— *What?*

— *They're Rmoahals. Over there. Rmoahals. It's all going to be fine.*

— *Sorry? Umrowa—?*

— *Tell you later. We're going to say hi.*

May takes her companion's hand again and they stand up straight and take several steps towards the fire. The men and women look up with no more than mild interest.

May raises her hand. calls something out.

— *What do we do?* whispers the dark-haired woman.

— *Follow my lead, OK.*

— *But what——?*

May, still looking intently towards the campfire, puts her finger to her lip.

One of the women steps to the edge of the circle of firelight. She gives no sign that she is surprised, or even curious. Her stance is, in some strange way, formal.

May steps forward to meet the giant woman.

— *Though we have intruded, we will respect your circle,* she says. She is apologetic. *We are lost.*

She offers the giant the palm of her hand, and the giant, squinting, leans forward to inspect it.

— *Eat with us.* The giant's vowels are distended, the consonants pushed to the front of the palate.

— *We're grateful,* says May. She glances meaningfully at her companion.

— Oh. Yeah. Thank you. Really.

The woman puts a long-fingered hand on her chest. *Chelié.*

— *I'm May.*

May turns to her companion, who gets the hint, and names herself. *Sarah.*

Chelié turns without any more introduction, and sits in the circle, leaving a space for May and Sarah, and, motioning the dark-haired woman to sit down first, May takes her place.

Some of the men, are toasting bread, roughly cut crusty white bread of the sort you get in the bakery counter from Tesco, over the fire.

One of them hands a couple of slices to May's host, who hands them in turn to May and Sarah.

— *I'm not hungry,* says Sarah.

— *You kind of need to be,* says May. She smiles brightly at Chelié and takes a bite.

After having finished her potato, May reaches up and touches Chelié's arm.

— *Thank you. We're sisters now.* May takes off her watch and offers it to Chelié, who grunts, and holds it up in the firelight, and regards it appreciatively.

May looks expectantly at Sarah. *Gift*, she says under her breath.

Sarah reaches up and undoes the buckle fastening the spiked collar around her neck. She reaches across May — May can feel Sarah's breath on her cheek, briefly, feels a sense of déja vu, understands a sort of intentionality, a question — and offers it. Chelié takes it, turns it over in her fingers and straps it onto a wrist already laden with bangles and beads.

One of the men whistles, and the women and the giant turn. More toast.

— *You hungry?* says May, not looking at Sarah.

— *Starving.*

— *Good.*

They sit for a while. The Rmoahal women talk among themselves about their menfolk, their families, their children. They make inexplicable jokes, references to things May and Sarah cannot understand. Their laughs are great bellows of amusement, heads thrown back, mouths — full of filed and dyed teeth — wide. May and Sarah have nothing to add, and no leave to add it.

And the men poke the fire and make toast.

10

May puts a hand gently on Chelié's thigh.

— *Thank you for making us so welcome. But we have to get home.*

— *Where?*

— *Acton.*

Chelié nods and whistles through those pointed teeth. A man, acquiline, face long and narrow like it's been stretched, looks up.

— *Moh. Hey. Moh. They have to get to Acton.*

— *Wife.* The man picks up his jingling spear and stands. He cocks his raw-boned head and looks at May and Sarah.

— *Time to go,* says May. She gets up, offers Sarah a hand. They stand for a second, facing each other, still holding hands.

May turns around. Standing, she is eye to eye with the seated Chelié.

— *Sisters,* says May. *You are owed.*

Chelié bares her teeth.

— *Sisters.*

Chelié's husband takes a few steps out of the ring of firelight, stops, looks back over his shoulder at the two women.

— We need to follow him, says May. *Don't talk to him, though. It's not the way.*

— I don't know who — what?

— They're the survivors of Atlantis. Or the last inhabitants of Eden, the ones who stayed when Adam and Eve were ejected from a state of grace. Or something. It amounts to the same thing, really. The point is, that they never lost their state of grace. They never had much of a fall. They might have tripped a bit. But that's about it.

— All of that stuff is made-up, though.

— Yep. They're wholly fictional. Completely made-up.

— Except they're not.

— We live in an interesting sort of world.

Sarah squeezes May's hand, and smiles.

They turn a corner around a vast block of polished basalt and the waste ground is gone; they're at the end of the back lane next to Acton Town tube station. As May and Sarah walk onto the street, Moh steps to one side, and then vanishes the way he came, without a word.

— How far is it to yours? says May.

— Three miles. Bit more.

— You can crash at mine if you like. I'm just around the corner. Got the time?

— Half past four.

— Crash at mine. Yeah.

It's only a couple hundred yards to May's house. It's only two turns away from the main road and the tube station, but Hillcrest Road is completely different in atmosphere:

small, neat houses with paths and gates and front gardens. Parked cars that never seem to go anywhere.

May pauses before she opens her front door.

— *Is everything OK?* says Sarah.

May looks over her shoulder at the house across the road, wonders if, just for a second, she glimpsed those same aged fingers at the edge of a curtain.

— *Fine. I'm fine.*

She opens the door and finds the light switch on the third try.

— *Get you a drink?* says May. *Tea? Coffee?*

— *Tea would be lovely.*

— *Kitchen's this way.*

They make for the kitchen; Sarah leans against the worktop as May empties the kettle, refills it, plugs it in, turns it on, finds a couple of mugs, teabags, the pot. And then May stops and leans forward, both hands on the counter, stares at the warming kettle. She closes her eyes and sighs.

Sarah is standing behind May; her hand touches the small of May's back. May jumps, breathes in once, hard, turns around. And now Sarah is reaching up, standing on tiptoe, palms against May's shoulders, kissing her.

May finds herself kissing back for a moment, and then she draws back and takes three uneven, ragged breaths in succession.

— *I don't — I'm not — I didn't —*

Sarah removes her hands from May's shoulders. The oily taste of her lipstick. The sweetness of bread and alcohol. The lingering odour of a single cigarette, hours ago.

— I'm sorry, she says.

She bites her lip, catching the little ball on her lip ring between her teeth, but she continues to look straight in May's eye. The kettle boils, clicks off.

— *No,* says May, *don't be. It's really nice, but —*

— *Would you like to do it again?*

May's diaphragm pulses; the fluttering in her chest. Imaginal giants, changing terrain, all these things she can navigate; this, this is too much.

Alcohol. Lipstick. Toasted bread.

— *Um.*

She looks to one side.

— *Yes,* she says.

0

I dreamed about May — not by name, she had a different name, but it was her — and she was not in the dream, except in the background, glimpsed from the corner of the eye.

There is a room in the dream, in May's house, in which some photos of and by May were hung. Sarah had seen May, confident, wise, magical, and had developed a crush on her. Sarah knows, too, from simple observation that May, knowing Ana too well, has been unable to make, that Ana is in love with May, but nonetheless Sarah asks Ana if she can get May's attention. She says she is too afraid to talk to May directly, but she does not say that she and May have already spent a night together. Ana shrugs.

— *I don't know,* she says.

Sarah does this: the second night she spends in May's house, she takes a picture of herself standing beside one of May's photographs, looking quizzically into the camera. And the third night they spend together, she replaces one of May's own pictures with this one. May does not notice, but she begins for reasons she cannot understand, to obsess over Sarah. It becomes, in the dream, more than a fling borne of fear and exhaustion. A few days later, Ana sees Sarah again, sitting on a park bench in what seems like some kind of cave, or maybe a waxworks museum.

Sarah asks Ana how she can avoid seeing May again. Something has happened between them, she says. Now May is pursuing Sarah, she says to Ana, and Sarah tells Ana she does not want May's attention. She has seen something in May, she tells Ana, knowing full well what this is doing to May's friend, that repels her. Sarah sees May coming, out of the corner of her eye, and asks Ana to make an excuse. She leaves the area. I, the unseen witness, the reason for them being here, leave too, and I move on to another dream, that I do not remember.

Stormboy

Abstract

You may not remember Stormboy.[1]

But at the time, it was a thing, and if I were to play it you, and you were here at a certain time, you'd know the song immediately, oh that song, the one you don't know the name of or who it's by but you know it can sing along with a line or two, imagine that somebody famous did the song but it was no one that you'd ever heard of, not even at the time.

It was the finest single ever made.[2]

If you weren't there, if you missed the Britpop thing because you wanted to avoid it or you were just too young, and someone tried to hum it to you or sing you a line, you would be forgiven for not knowing what the fuss is about.

The chords are only obvious, the playing not particularly great; the lead vocalist cannot really sing. No one who covered it ever got past the limitations of the song.

But the single itself joins all its strengths and weaknesses into something inexplicable and sublime; it speaks of hope and disappointment, loneliness, desertion and grief and the way we sometimes try to reach beyond these things

---

1   "Stormboy" was a UK Top Ten hit for the Herons for one
    week in August 1997.
2   In 2001, *Mojo* magazine listed "Stormboy" as no.16 in its list
    of the Greatest Singles of All Time. It does not appear in any
    subsequent or prior versions of the list.

and find contentment in them; I cannot ever do it justice. My voice is not enough.

I can't sing it to you.

And it felt like Sunday

And I called myself a stormboy

A battered and forlorn boy...

I can't even remember the next line.

I knew the Herons. I was at university with them, Adam, Ryan, Gwen and... you know.[3]

Why this one song should have been so utterly sublime; why they never made another half as good; why now they are only three. It's a mystery. It's all a mystery.

i. A College

Out above the backend of the Uplands[4], one street up the hill from Ffynone school, there's a lane, down which hardly anyone goes these days. At its end, behind a run-down rusty fence and a row of overgrown trees is a large abandoned building, with five wings, built in a mid-Victorian Gothic style. It used to be a college of the University of Wales; some nights, it still is.

At certain times during the year, on varying nights in varying months, but always when the moon is clear in the sky half-full, the empty building develops a covering of frost. Through long-deserted office windows, august

---

3   The surviving members of the Herons are Adam Lockwood, Gwen Colley and Ryan Hood.

4   We are talking about Swansea.

academics can be seen shuffling papers, reading books, writing treatises.

It is July. It's been a brutal month, a hundred degrees or more every day this week, but around the college, it is always raining. Walking up the path, stepping inside, I nearly slip on the rain-slick algae-covered stones.

The corridor is lit with a naked electric lightbulb. I can hear a voice coming from the third door on the right.

Peeking round the door, I see a class full of students, taking notes from a lecture, given by a tall, thin man with bottle-bottom glasses pushed right up to the top of his nose.

There are other rooms: more lectures, offices in which elderly men and women sit alone at desks surrounded by notes and dusty quartos.

Everything is covered with rain, or algae or mould. The staff, are caked with rain, algae and mould, their smell metallic and cold, their clothes squelching as they move, leaving greenish snailtrails on the furniture as their writing wrists move across the tables, shift on the lecture benches. No one shivers; only my breath is visible.

The last room on the corridor is a departmental office. The near-skeletal, colourless, cobweb-draped woman behind the desk smiles with an audible creak, nods, hands me a schedule of courses and lectures.

I flip through the phone-book sized catalogue, as I wander through the winding, infinite corridors of the building, squinting at minuscule text.

Every subject, no matter how apparently insignificant, is important, worthy of study; every dream, every whim, every conversation is worth thinking about, every life's story is material for any number of essays and theses. [5]

I walk randomly through the department's corridors for an hour or more, not really feeling the cold, poring through the list — arranged in the order the lectures are given, rather than on their subjects, somewhat frustratingly. After a while, I become aware that I've been walking all this time. I look up from the course catalogue.

I'm next to a door, covered in chipped blue paint. Screwed on at eye level is a sign: *Thesis Store.*

My curiosity gets the better of me. No one's around, and the door is unlocked.

I step inside, leaving a little cloud of breath behind me.

So. The thesis store is a massive room, far too big for the building. Lit dimly by naked yellow lightbulbs, library stacks stretch off for what seems like miles in every direction, receding into shadow before anything like a far wall is reached.

I shrug — nothing ventured — and start on the stack immediately in front of me, brushing past a spider's web,

---

5   A representative sample from the course and seminar list:

An examination of the adolescent dreams of Martin Suggs, mechanic, West Woolwich.

The movements of aphids in the garden of Freda West, Brynmill, Swansea.

Exegesis of a domestic contretemps between Mr and Mrs A. Scott, High Street, Durham.

A reader-response criticism of the book Iris Page (Pennycross, Plymouth) wanted to write, but never got round to completing.

The dreams of pop idoldom of Jade Wright, nine-year-old, Selly Oak, Birmingham.

which flickers in the low light, strewn with tiny crystalline drops.

My search is complicated by the cataloguing system — the theses are alphabetised by author. Damn. Still. The possibility of hitting on what I want to know, although minute, is still there and so I decide to carry on anyway.

One thesis catches my eye: *The Circumstances Surrounding the Accidental Death of Mark Dingle and its Effects on the Unity of His Family.* J. Desult, PhD, 1999.

I knew a kid called Mark Dingle at school. I flip through, looking for facts. Yes, it was the same one. He'd been hit by a car the day before his university graduation, up in Leeds. I didn't know he was dead. I didn't even know he had gone to University in Leeds.

I started around "D", and after two hours of scouring the stacks, I am still on "D". My watch says it's about 3am now. I'm just about ready to give up when I see another one that rings a bell.

Stormboy. A.P. Doyer, PhD. 2001.

This one I take out and open.

My fingers are now so numb with the cold, I can barely turn the flyleaf.

Inside is the full title: *Stormboy: The Success and Failure of the Herons' Debut Single and the Subsequent Breakup of the Band.* A. P. Doyer, PhD 2001.

Not exactly what I was looking for, but... things I want to know about. I give up on my other search.

No one else will be reading this particular essay any time soon, so I decided to borrow it. I tuck it under my arm and stroll nonchalantly out of the thesis store, and then find my way out of the college and into the early morning rain.

ii. A Pub

That night, Simon and I headed up to the Uplands Tavern. It was not normally a destination of ours, it being — and I'm aware of the irony – too full of students.

We managed to find a place to stand as the Herons — Adam (rhythm guitar and vocals), Ryan (drums), Gwen (bass and vocals) and, yeah. We find a place as they set up.[6]

When they finally came on, ten minutes late — Gwen, apparently, had a fight with Adam over some leads — they got only a smattering of applause.

They were good. Jangly sweet. Electric ringing.[7] Adam was miked up high; you can hear every word. The songs, they were OK. Songs about people our age being lonely or miserable or not getting laid. Slow verses, choruses that rose.

Adam's voice, a clear tenor, sang the notes he gave himself, no histrionics.

More people listened, took notice; more applause throughout the evening, although the biggest applause came from a not-entirely-successful attempt to do that Stone Roses song with the five-minute guitar solo. Adam spoke, thanked the audience.

"This is going to be our last song tonight. I wrote this one last week. It's called Stormboy."

And I asked to be martyred. Politely
Put up my fists, told them to fight me.

---

6   May 1995, this was.

7   Artists the Herons liked: The Stone Roses; The Beatles; Gorky's Zygotic Mynci; Catatonia; Nick Drake; The La's (only Adam); REM (only Ryan); U2 (all of them, but none of them admitted it).

104

My bruises aren't so bad.

It follows the same formula as all the others, but somehow these things all come together. The words aren't especially good, the melody is really no more catchy than any of their others.

The cumulative effect of the song — its bland lyrics, its pedestrian tune, the performance of the band, particularly the lead guitar, his performance that makes so much sense now — is still the same. It tugs at you, a dreadful, clutching, lonely sadness that fills you up.[8]

Every single person in the pub — every single person — stopped what they were doing, listened.[9]

It takes you too long to get just what that means

When nothing ever changes, except the cut of your jeans[10]

The last chord rang out, echoed across the bar, faded into silence. No one moved, said anything. The band stood, unaware of what has just happened — what just happened? I didn't know.

---

8   When "Stormboy" was first played on the BBC Radio 1 Breakfast Show in January 1997, DJ Chris Evans famously left thirty seconds of dead air immediately following the song. Apparently, this incident contributed to his decision to leave the show within the next few weeks.

9   A man sat with his hand on his mouth. A young woman by the bar with pink hair stood enthralled, unaware that she had dropped her pint, that it had smashed all over the floor. The bar help — a skinny boy in a Guinness T-shirt, leant on the bar as if that was all that was holding him up, crying. Lager stopped halfway to mouths.

10 David Balfe's label Food Records (most famous labelmates: Blur) signed the Herons in February 1996.

They stood, confused, in a whole minute of silence. Simon stood up then, started to applaud and whoop, and I took the clue, joined in. One or two began to applaud. Most people were quiet. It died.

They left the mic then, Adam, Ryan, Gwen and... Yes. Conversation arose again, subdued, forced, awkward, about anything except that last song played by the band.

Adam and Gwen came to sit with us. Adam was apologetic, almost.

"I don't know what happened. It was never like that when we rehearsed it."

Have you played that last one live before?

"No. This is the first time we've done that one in front of an audience. It died on its arse. "

"No," said Simon. "No, mate. You've got it all wrong, you have. That wasn't everyone hating it, see. That, man, was the best thing that I or anyone else in this fine drinking establishment have ever heard."

"Fuck off."

"No, man. I'm serious. You have to play that one again. You have to."[11]

iii. An Angel

It is the first time I've darkened the doors of a church since the funeral.

And today the reading is the first part of Matthew 18. Verse ten, as always, draws my attention, although I know

---

11 When it crashed, the radio in Princess Diana's car was tuned to a station that had just played "Stormboy".

that the vicar, good Protestant that he is, will not address it in his sermon.

See that you do not look down on these little ones. For I tell you that their angels in heaven always see the face of my Father in heaven.[12]

I never used to think too hard about that. The guardian angels, I mean. Does everyone have them? Are they all so efficient? Do they all do their job adequately?[13]

I forget when I found out that my own angel's name is Daniel. He lost his faith some time ago. Maybe he wanted to do more than he could and fell short of his goals. Maybe he felt that circumstances thwarted his attempts to prosper and protect me. Maybe he was just lazy, but couldn't see that, blaming everything but his own inaction. Did he do enough? I don't know.

I imagine him as being like me, trying, but not trying too hard, bewailing the lack of breaks he got, the lack of opportunities which he really has no right to expect. Like me. Like Stormboy, flawed and perfect and marred by death and pain.

It came on the radio again this morning, as if to remind me of him, remind me that I am here to say goodbye.

And it felt like Sunday

And I called myself a Stormboy

And God said you weren't born boy

Daniel began to doubt his place and he began to doubt whether God had given him the power to achieve anything. And he achieved nothing. He began to wonder

12 Matthew, 10:18.

13 The *qashmallim* are the fourth choir of angels, according to Christian mythology.

if he was just unlucky, surely a hard thing for an angel born into the sure knowledge of the providence of God to come to believe. But he did. He began to think that no justice could exist. He began to think that God either couldn't do anything or didn't care and wouldn't.

I don't know if Daniel is right. But right doesn't have much to do with these things. Daniel lost his faith in himself, and then he lost his faith in God.

Oh no, you're thinking, oh no, an angel can't lose his faith in God, because where would that leave us?

And if you're more theologically inclined, you're thinking, how can this happen?

An angel has no free will. If an angel loses his faith, who can be responsible for that but God?

I don't know about the theology of it. It wasn't too long ago that it was all sure and sorted in my own head. Now I don't know. But I know that Daniel made his own decision. No one compelled him. His failure to achieve was his own doing. His doubts were his own, and his loss of faith "that was his own.

Daniel didn't notice when he fell. I don't think he knows when it happened, just that one day he realised that God began to give him no time, no help, no notice, and that his praises to the Almighty began to be rote and parroted and empty. He had lost his faith and he fell. But he was still my angel, and he is still my angel now. He just carried on doing his job. He takes no joy in the work. But there is nothing else for him to do.

He walks back streets, the endless back lanes of my town, humming Stormboy to himself.

He's still in denial, really. He can't bring himself to look in the mirror most mornings. He can't bring himself to take note of the way that the feathers on both pairs of wings have become charred and greasy like a well-used grill pan, and he won't acknowledge that the teeth in the mouth of his calf's head have become sharp and yellow.

Daniel still writes to his colleagues. He never saw them much to begin with, and they communicated a lot through letters. He writes to them now of his fears and the doubts which consume him. They don't write back any more. But he keeps on writing. He posts on Twitter. He leaves messages on walls.

("Dear Uriel,

I sometimes wonder why so much of what happens to the people we're supposed to guard is so bad. Why are we so ineffectual?")

He saw one of his colleagues a few weeks ago, in the distance, all light and halo and shining wings, looking down benevolently on his sleeping charge. Daniel looked down at himself and fingered one of his feathers, and he felt it come away in his hand, and he looked at it, and it was all black and filthy. He held it in a bony black-nailed hand that he couldn't recognise as his own. So he hid. He ran away before the angel could see him.

Daniel has begun to find other people to blame. He has begun to wonder if this was my fault. He has begun to wonder if I'm not a hopeless case.

He is gradually beginning to hate me. If I won't be helped, then why not just make me go down the path that I was always destined to do? So now he nudges my elbow. He tells me things to make me doubt myself and make me doubt my faith.

109

And he kept me self-obsessed, so that I could not see that my friend was in need. So that I would blame myself when we all had to arrange a funeral, and it was too late.

He thinks it's all my fault, you see. But it isn't.

I think that maybe we deserve each other.

Summary Statement

There are no explanations, for any of this, only things we cannot bring ourselves to say. Songs we cannot sing.

Pillar of salt

For the longest time, this pillar of salt has been a landmark. I have, it goes without saying, visited it myself. It stands on the side of the hill of limestone and salt on the corner of the Dead Sea, overlooking the plain, vaguely human in aspect. Shoulders. Half of a head if you look at it from some angles. It's maybe thirty feet tall. It used to look more like a human, be smaller, but the salt from the saturated breeze builds up over the centuries, has collected around it, made it higher, wider. Lot's Wife, they call it.

I remember standing in the evening sunlight — I still remember sunlight; why would I deny that? — in the stripes of red and orange light, and breathless from the climb I put the palm of my had against it and felt the roughness and dryness of the salt against my skin, felt it almost leach away the sweat. I imagined I heard, deep inside, a scream.

I snatched my hand away, looked at the tiny crumbs of red-brown rocksalt attached to my palm. Then I brushed them away, urgently rubbing the hand on my pants.

A very old manuscript fragment, Greek and Syriac, had passed into my hands. I had acquired it a few days before from an artifact seller down in Cairo, one of those men who scour the detritus of the petrified rubbish dump at Oxyrhynchus for treasures before the archaeologists get there, a little goat of a man, I remember, with round, wide-set eyes and a sparse tuft on his chin.

He asked for American dollars for it, eight hundred. It is so ancient, he said, and important.

I said, eight hundred for this old scrap? Look, it has nothing of value on it. Two hundred.

See how dense this writing is, how much is there, he said. I would not part with it for less than seven.

And so on. He got me to five hundred and fifty. I would have given thousands for it.

You think we dig for our finds?

The draft of a letter in Greek is on one side, three times, not terribly of interest, family news. My children are well, my daughter is of marriageable age, and so is your son, and would you consider a match, the sort of thing that people would draft on the cut up scraps of old books, papyrus being what it was. The Syriac, though, cramped and crabbed and minute, full of holes, there is the interest. The man didn't know. But he saw the light go on in my eyes. Those five hundred and fifty dollars American probably meant he could have a holiday.

It must, I have surmised, have been part of some miscellany. A book of traveller's tales, perhaps, or a collection of wonders of the sort that grew in popularity during the later Roman Empire, Like the *Florida*, perhaps, or one of the *Geographies*. This part, beginning mid-sentence, describes the pillar of salt it as it was in the time of the Israelite Kings. In the story, it was about six feet high. It used to have an eyeless, noseless face, turned as if looking over a pair of shoulders, and a round hole like a mouth, that seemed to have a terrible darkness inside it, which screamed when the wind blew, high-pitched, grieving, the mindless howl of one who could do no other than stand and lament forever.

The fragment describes how a traveller, a Greek of the time of Kleisthenes, visited the pillar, and found that he could not bear to hear the pillar screaming in the wind. He took an axe, the fragment say, took an axe and knocked the head clean off, and the clouds boiled red in the low afternoon and sticky trickles of blood ran from the parts of the rock formation that suggested a neck and down the side of the pillar, the smell of salt and sweat and metal in the air that hung in the back of the man's throat.

The fragment says that the traveller was offered no respite, but — and it cuts off there, end of a page, story unfinished.

I imagine the nameless traveller there, looking down at the eyeless face on the ground, with its gaping round darkness, still screaming up at him, the howling still audible above the Canaanite wind. I imagine him returning to his lodging, twisting in the dark on the rope-sprung bed, the dust vibrating with the scream from an eyeless face.

He returns to the pillar the next day, axe in hand, intending to smash the face to dull brown rock-salt shards. It is of course gone; the pillar has grown, has lost definition, become colossal, looks like rocksalt, nothing more. The scream continues, over the whistle of the evening wind. Red sky. Boiling, roiling clouds. He clutches the sides of his head, the axe falling to the ground, the bronze head clanging against the rock, harmonizing with the endless scream. He walks, as if shoved by an insistent hand, down to the Dead Sea, into the buoyant waters, and walks, until the waters buoy him up, and he floats face down on the surface, until the screaming stops.

•

Among the more obscure of the lesser *midrashim*, the apocrypha of the apocryphal, you can find this story. Here is Abraham the Patriarch, alone, sitting cross-legged on a mountainside, and he is waiting to begin a conversation.

He will come up here quite soon and prove that he is a man obedient enough to agree to murder his own begging, crying child on a word, but this comes before that particular story. It comes after the story where, named only Abram, he stands on a plain and is told his descendants will outnumber the stars by the same voice that will tell him to murder his son; that one is significant to this account, because of the way this particular version of the story is told.

In that version, Abram stands alone and it is as if the wilderness becomes a threshing floor and great bronze-handled grindstones, as if from some colossal mill, descend and rise, two pairs from the sky, two pairs from the earth, the base of each inscribed with one letter of a language he cannot read, one letter of the Tetragrammaton, the Name. And it is as if he sees the inner workings of the world. Each of the grindstone pairs has a voice, or part of a voice, made from the rasping impact of stone on stone, inhuman, implacable. In unison they call his name. The noise of that one word is more than his body can take, and blood begins to flow from his ears, his eyeballs, his nose. But he cannot move, cannot even fall to the ground and when the rotating stones descend upon him and draw him in, blind, deaf, mad, by the corner of his robe and grind him into paste he can only allow it. He doesn't even scream.

And the stones rise into the air and descend into the earth and the ground opens into an oven and from the oven, like a clay pot comes Abraham, replaced, remade inside and out, working sperm in his testes and a brain reordered to accept the word of the stones. Ready to be father of a line whose traces will exist in three thousand

114

years in every human in Europe and the Middle East. Ready to obey the Name.

And it is this Abraham, crafted from raw material called Abram, soon to get a new name to go with his new mind and his new body, who sits on the mountain waiting for the stones to come and grind out the words he will obey, the Bronze-Age nomad crafted as an early component in a machine of history.

The stones come from the sky and rise from the ground around him, and he does not bleed for inside he is as much leather and bronze and rocksalt as he is man and he clicks and asks what the stones will of him. And in the low rumbling, the grindstones tell him that it serves that Sodom and Gomorrah will be destroyed.

Abraham is still, the text explains, though obedient and remade, a man, and he bargains with the grindstone Tetragrammaton. His nephew, Lot, lives in Sodom. He states the logic that this man is his family, and hence protected, for the Name cannot be inconsistent. He asks, are there fifty men who would be worth serving the Name? And the stones descend into the ground and rise into the sky, and all is quiet for a time; and presently they return and say that no, fifty men worthy of being remade as Abram cannot be found.

And so Abraham asks if there are forty, and again the stones withdraw, and return, and respond in the negative, as they do when he asks if the city of Sodom houses thirty worthy men, as they do when he asks if the city has twenty, as they do when he asks if the city has ten.

Then the stones say that Lot will be saved for Lot is of his line and part of the Principle of History, and Abraham accepts, and the stones tell him to go home, and he does, for he obeys the Name. He has been made to obey.

So much for the part of Abraham in this story. This particular midrash has much to say of him, and of his descendants (its version of the Ladder of Jacob is worth an essay of its own) but here we concentrate on Sodom. We concentrate on Lot.

The canonical Bible (and it is worth remembering that no one authority decided on the Bible canon we have — we naturally chose that version that comforted us, that frightened us the least) has Abraham asking the Name to find righteous men, good men. And no, God can't find ten good men. And this is important, because the Bible does not tell us that God can find any good men. Lot escapes because God had promised protected status to the family of Abraham. Lot, as even the canon tacitly accepts, is not a good man, as we will see.

So two nights hence, Lot receives visitors, he receives them because the grindstone Name has earmarked him as of the same blood — and the same raw material — as Abraham. The Name chooses to preserve him because of some character in his bloodline that suits the machine. That's all. Goodness, in this version of the tale, is not a consideration.

These two men have round, blank eyes of a deep blue, that glitter in the sunset like Egyptian faience. Their skin is dull and pale like doeskin, their faces like leather stretched over stone images. They have no hair. They wear no beard.

Lot sees them in the square. And something breaks in his brain. He goes outside.

Come. Eat with me.

We will stay in the square. The man's voice grinds. It shrieks.

He repeats himself. Come. Eat with me.

Lot takes the strangers in. has his slaves wash their feet, offers them wine, which they do not drink, and bread and freshly killed lamb, which they do not eat. They sit around the fire, and his wife, his sons-in-law and his twin daughters, none of them permitted names in this or any other version, sit beside them at the table as the slaves of the house, taken from far away, serve food uneaten.

A slave boy looks too hard at the face of one of the strangers and cries out; his hand shakes and the wine spills. Lot backhands him so suddenly and so hard he falls to the ground and his head bounces off the stone, and he crawls to the room whimpering. The host apologises, and the twin daughters, nameless in this version of the story as in all the others glance at each other and then look at their mother, who averts her eyes from them and, unconsciously, pulls her robe closer around herself, as if to conceal the discoloured patches of skin on her chest, on her throat.

Lot apologises to the strangers for the carelessness of his property and assures them that he will punish the slave himself. For their part, the strangers ignore that the incident ever happened, and unison explain that the Name will destroy Sodom, Gomorrah and the surrounding cities of the plain, for they have no suitable material; Lot and his daughters have the correct material in their bodies and they must leave.

What of his sons-in-law?

They are not the correct material. They will die.

Lot's wife keeps her silence. The sons-in-law protest, loudly, declare it an insult. Lot never really liked them

117

anyway, considers his dowry wasted. He laughs in their faces. The two men storm out of the house. Lot's unnamed daughters do not try to stop them.

The screeching voice of the blank-eyed strangers continues: they must prepare to leave, the three of them, for destruction will come this very night. Lot snaps his fingers and tells his wife to prepare provisions for him and his daughters, suitable for the farthest trip they can. Knowing his humours, the younger women do not object, but they share looks with their mother, and she nods, and they go to help her, leaving their father alone with the strangers.

I will come, she says. I will not leave you alone with him.

In the other room, she packs for four. In her own bag, she packs a knife.

Lot sits with the strangers. You have the blood of Abraham, one says.

Lot wipes a trickle of blood from his nose, stares at it. My uncle is no friend, he says.

The dull-skinned men stare at him with their unblinking faience eyes. You will leave, they say. Leave the plain this night.

It isn't possible, he says. I wouldn't be able to get further than Zoar.

You will go to Zoar, then.

Lot cannot engage them on any other subject of conversation; they speak of the urgency of leaving, and they will oversee the escape of Lot and his daughters, and only those three.

The girls in the other room quietly, frantically plot with their mother; Lot will not make it as far as they do.

They will dispatch him in his sleep on that first night and travel to Zoar — it is as far as they can travel reasonably, they decide — as widows, and there they will survive by gleaning the corn, which is the right of the widow, and will be better than a life in Sodom with Lot. It will be better than a life anywhere with Lot.

A tumult outside. The sounds of chanting, shouting. Lot comes to the door. Men, thirty, forty. Lot's sons-in-law at their head. They are reeling, slurring, wine stains down the front of their robes.

Lot has stolen their wives. Lot has listened to strangers, outsiders. Lot, also a little drunk by now, yells back. They are his guests. His right of hospitality. A fleck of Lot's spittle lands on the forehead of one of the sons-in-law.

Bring them out, shouts someone in the crowd. Bring the outsiders. Give us the outsiders. You've taken my brother's wife from him, so give us them instead. We'll all make wives of them. The midrash doesn't spell out what the other men are shouting now, only that it quickly becomes obscene, threatening.

Lot is silent. He becomes aware that the strangers are standing behind him. He is quieter now, regains a little dignity.

You can't have them.

We're not going, says a man in the crowd. We'll be satisfied.

I'm obligated, says Lot. Hospitality. They've got my hospitality.

Take my daughters, says Lot. You can have my daughters. If these two want them, fine. You can all have them.

119

(The nineteenth chapter of *Genesis* does not disagree on this point.)

He turns, meaning to drag the girls out and throw them to the mob. The strangers block his way.

The women inside, their bundles packed, hearing this, seethe, shake. One of the daughters starts to reach for the knife; her mother puts her hand over the girl's. Not now. We'll have him. But not now.

One of the men says to Lot in that grinding, screeching voice, You and your daughters will leave now, by the back. Lot can see a crack across the faience glaze of the stranger's round, empty eye.

The strangers walk out past Lot, shoulder past him like they're stone, into the crowd. The light of torches reflects on their skin, their faience eyes. Someone reaches forward to grab a shoulder, and the stranger's robe falls off and the skin of his shoulder with it, and both men, in front of Lot's terrified, blurred eyes, somehow unfold into something of bronze and stone. The reaching hand, still grasping the stranger's skin, gains a spreading covering of white-brown rocksalt, and then breaks off at the elbow, crumbles, blows away on the wind.

The strangers or the things that were the strangers are huge now, shapeless conglomerations of brass blades and wooden posts and granite stones that tower over the panicked crowd that reduce men to crumbling salt statues with a touch, that stamp on men and crush them to a pulp unawares, that drag them screaming into grindstones and reduce them to paste, just as Abram was, but bring nothing back.

Lot looks for a moment, and then turns, rushes through the house headlong, to the rear room, the women's

120

room, screams at his daughters in a way that he has never screamed at them before in the most drunken of furies, and the four of them, the man and the three women, Lot's wife allowed to come because in the panic Lot does not think to forbid her.

They do not look back, do not stop running, stumbling, pressing on; around them great machined stones rain from the sky, wreathed in flame, which then, grotesquely, *stand up* and walk through the streets, touching, treading, crushing.

A dog runs headlong into them almost, stops dead, its yelps cut short as it becomes salt and crumbles in the wind. A house collapses across their path in flames, its occupants' cries of anguish cut short, cut dead. One of Lot's daughters says, the slaves.

Damn the slaves.

They double back, noting that their house has already gone. Around them walking things of stones and bronze crush and grind, reduce houses to dust, liquefy men and women who although flesh rather than stone cannot outrun the Name's monolithic agents, who perform their task without anything resembling wrath, in this version of the story at least.

Outside of the city walls, which they hear crumbling behind them, though they do not look back, the plain shakes. They cross a narrow crack in the earth that behind them opens up into a chasm the moment they pass it. A stream nearby bubbles and hisses and boils away. They can hear the salt sea, miles away, complaining, bringing an unaccustomed storm to bear. Everything is tumult. Ears ring. Heads pound.

121

And now up the great rock overlooking the plain, and the women and Lot breathe a sigh of relief, and fall to their knees on the stone.

They can hear the screams from the cities of the plain behind, as if the women and the children, the animals and the slaves, cry out in unison as the messengers of the Name erase them from the earth in fire and gravel and salt. Ground into nothing.

And then the screams stop, and the roaring of stones. And the noise subsides, leaving the loudest thing the ringing of ears. Everything smells of salt and sulphur. It's on their clothes, on their tongues, in the dust coating their skin.

None of them look back. And then a voice, grinding, screeching. Three of you are to be saved.

Lot is on his hands and knees, staring at the ground. His wife begins to cry, his daughters holding each other's hands, wide-eyed, breathing heavily, more horror etched on faces that thought they couldn't see any more. Something snaps, something behind the eyes.

None of them turn around.

No noise now, no sound save the far-off crackle of fire and sulphur in the distance. None of them turn around still. A minute passes, or an hour. The first ray of sunlight flashes over the ridge.

The tension passes. Slowly, the twins' mother turns round, glances over her shoulder.

A creak, like stone cracking. And then nothing.

A sound of something vanishing, withdrawing.

A pillar of salt, shaped roughly as a human, its eyeless noseless face devoid of any feature save a deep black maw, like a mouth caught in a scream.

•

Zoar is a full day and a night away on foot.

The news got there first on horseback; a scout, a watcher, and plumes of smoke in the distance.

They barely get past the outer circle of the settlement before the first stone lands in front of their feet, a warning shot. Men and women advancing in rows now. No one from Sodom is going to come here. Not now. Not with the curse of the city rising in the sky behind them, black and glowering.

Back to the rock is the only place left to go. No one talks. The girls, younger, fitter, stay out of the old man's reach. Only a couple of the flailing blows from his stick land, enough for his daughters to descend into wordless plans, silent exchanges of glances beneath knitted brows.

The cave is dry; hollow white needle-thin stalactites hang in clusters from the ceiling. The floor marks their filthy robes and near-worn through sandals with white.

He sits against the crumbling wall, and rants. He is ruined. He has no son, no heir, only these useless daughters, who could not give him grandchildren, who did not understand discipline. They brought the curse down on him. His uncle brought the curse down. His wife brought the curse down, she never should have left with them.

He can't stand. He can barely raise his staff to swing feebly at them. Oh, but when he gets his strength back, then they'll know, then he'll beat them to death and die here himself. He takes the wineskin and drains it. He falls into a stupor.

Soon he is lying on his back.

The girls look at each other.

Slowly, Lot's two daughters begin to undress him.

•

He sleeps for another day and another night and if it looks like he'll wake they ply him with more wine, and one time when he tries to open his eyes they batter him over his head with a piece of rocksalt that shatters against his skull and leaves its remains in his matted hair, glued in place with the dark trickle of blood born of the impact.

And the two nameless sisters cry out with a kind of wild-eyed glee as they take their revenge against him.

When he finally wakes, he knows. He knows. He is red-eyed, aghast, silent. And they are there, as naked as he, on hands and knees, finishing each other's sentences. Now he has sons, oh yes, and they'll be the only sons he has, because no one will take him, knowing what he has done, and no one will ever take them either, they'll never have to be wives again and beaten again. For they are free now, and oh he is welcome to be the patriarch, but to strike them any more, to abuse them any more is the end of his line, they'll assure it, and the faience-eyed strangers wanted the line to carry on, didn't they, and oh, isn't he afraid of them, isn't he, isn't he, isn't he, and oh, here it is, here is the line, right here.

One rocks back on her haunches, points to her stomach. Here is your future, Lot, the future you wanted. The one you deserved.

Oh Father, you are ours now. Give us to the drunken mob, would you? Offer us up over strangers who would murder everything we ever loved? Oh Father, we are not even begun with you.

They advance on him, eyes feral beneath matted hair.

•

In the Bible canon, the editions that sit in church pews and which are never read in their entirety, the daughters of Lot rape their father for his own good. He needs a son, so they both take him, and he thanks them, and they found kingdoms apart from the Hebrew children of Abraham. The blood of Lot, I believe, is spread far now, and anyone of Middle Eastern or European descent probably has a trace of it.

I wonder what that means, as I read my papyrus genealogies, my Oxyrhynchus fragments, my apocryphal midrash. I wonder what sort of cull the Name may yet inflict on us, now there are so many more of us, and I wonder what kind of Machine that God is made of now, since the Bronze Age is so far behind us.

There are so many transformations a God like that might inflict upon the people of earth. There are so many deaths that the artifices of such a Tetragrammaton might bring.

I returned on three separate research trips to the site of Lot's Wife, hoping, perhaps, to find her face. I never found it, but as I placed my hand on the rock salt that last time, I heard it, on the wind, screaming. I closed my eyes. Opened them. It went away, I thought.

I took the scream home with me.

I can hear it now as I compile the papers, shuffle photographs of stones. I hear it still. It sings to my blood. I wonder how long it will be before I walk into the salt myself, and float face down until I am free.

An after-hours reading

You must be sincere with the Tarot in order for the Tarot to be sincere with you. This is why I insist — I insist! — that never mind how late it is, we shall do this properly. The formalities must be observed if you are to be open to its wisdom.

Here. Take the deck. No, you won't have to wash your hands. It's good to give a little of yourself to the cards. Stains on these cards have a way of fading, after all. Look at the cards. The Tarot is a lot like a deck of cards you might recognise, yes. Fifty-six cards in four suits, Pentacles rather than Diamonds, Cups instead of Hearts, Swords in the place of Spades, Wands for Clubs. Four Aces. Four sets of two through ten, Knights, Pages, Kings and Queens. Rather than one Joker, here are twenty-two Trump cards, each with its own name and own meaning. The Magician, the Hermit, the Tower, the Lovers, the Hanged Man, the Sun, Death.

Some call the Tarot the Book of Thoth — did you know that? — a repository of wisdom in a form of near-impenetrable complexity, visual, associative, anything but linear. Its combinations may not necessarily be infinite in any literal sense, but I can guarantee you that you will never in your lifetime, or a hundred more, exhaust its permutations. This is more than simple fortune telling. By laying out the cards of the Tarot, you lay out the past, the present and the future. You lay out your soul and your soul's fate in all its complexity, beauty and tragedy.

Bring yourself. Yes, yes, you're here, of course you are, but you know full well, dearie, that isn't what I mean. Be open! Be sincere. If you are sincere with the Tarot, as I said, the Tarot will be sincere with you.

As for the other things you bring, well. You won't need them. The knife, for example, is unnecessary. Keep it in sight, on the table between us if it makes you more comfortable.

We shall do the reading as if you were any normal client. We shall do it as if it were daylight, and you were paying. It's why you're here, isn't it? Of course it is.

Now. Every clairvoyant has their own way of laying out a Tarot spread. Mine is as traditional and as valid as any. No. You keep the deck. You must lay it out.

First. Separate the Trumps of the Major Arcana — the ones with Roman numerals and unique names — from the suited cards of the Minor Arcana, the Cups, Swords, Pentacles and Wands. Put the Minor cards to one side. We'll deal with them in a moment. Shuffle the Trumps.

I will of course watch you, yes. The effort into which you are putting into shuffling them is not only a mark of your character, it is a vital element. The more thoroughly you shuffle the cards, the more of yourself you will find there. Do not be lackadaisical. Be sincere.

Now. Cut them into three piles. Place the first on the second, the third on the first. From the top of this deck, deal yourself twelve cards, face up, as they come, in two rows of six, first the top row, then the bottom. Ah, no, don't rectify their positions if they come out upside down. It matters. Leave them as they are.

Now take the Minor Arcana and do the same. Shuffle them — inevitably you will shuffle them more thoroughly, for you have been made self-conscious. It's entirely human. Cut them in the same way, arrange the piles as you did before, and deal twelve cards over the others, covering them.

Now. Each of these twelve places deals with a different part of your past, and your present, and your future. And the first cards here, the ones on your top left, these are vital. They define you. They illuminate the question that brought you — ah, ah, no. No cheating. The cards will tell us the heart of the matter. You don't need to say.

Let us see.

Four of Cups, reversed:

A goddess, hips and breasts pendulous and fecund like a Willendorf Venus, stands atop what could be a flight of steps, or a ziggurat, balanced delicately on the tiptoes of one foot. On the step beneath her, four chalices stand, each half-full of milk. She stares at you, less than content.

In this place? It's about sex. Or love. But probably sex. Does that embarrass you? Why should it? Reversed, it suggests a relationship that has ended, or which is soon to end. Let us lift it, and see what lies beneath.

VI. The Lovers:

Two women, naked, embrace. One is stiff, bluish in hue, eyes closed. She might be tired, or dead. Her head rests on the shoulder of the other who, alert, stares at you, in accusation or challenge.

Ah, the Lovers. Not always about affairs of the heart, this. Traditionally, you have three figures on this card. They represent the three angels that magicians call the

Children of the Voice, Madriax, Peripsol and Gmicalzoma. Gmicalzoma appears to be absent today. How odd. No matter. The Lovers deals with a fateful decision primarily. How apt though, that it lie beneath a card that deals with the desires of the body.

From the first place in the reading, we cross to the seventh, beneath it, which stands in opposition to you. It is the space of relationships. Partnerships. Your heart in the world.

Eight of Swords:

A barren, rocky landscape. A hand, gnarled, scratched, protrudes from the earth, its owner presumably beneath, clawing for air, for freedom, for life. In the background, seven swords stand, thrust point-down into the earth; the shards of a broken eighth lie in the foreground.

Oh, I am afraid that the Eight of Swords is ill-omened. It speaks of ordeal, opposition. I think here it means that there is, or has been, some insoluble quarrel. Is that the case? You're looking at your hand, I see. It looks like your hand, doesn't it? Don't be unsettled, dearie. Perhaps the card it covers may yet overrule it.

XVI. The Tower:

The pinnacled spires of an ancient city stand on the shore, menaced by a tidal wave which stands, foaming, looming in the eternal moment of stillness that precedes its crashing down on the landscape below, destroying all before it. A tiny, lone figure cowers on the beach between the city and the wave, despairing, sure of imminent death.

Ah, no. Maybe not.

Perhaps the most ill-omened card in the entire deck, the Tower speaks of disaster. Your argument did not end well, did it? Still. The Tarot is not without hope. Who knows what mitigations our reading might bring you?

The second position, then. Money. The material.

Ten of Pentacles:

Ten large, round coins on a table, each inscribed with a five-pointed star. As you look, it seems that spots of red appear on them. You look at your hands.

You have come into some money. Whence might that be, I wonder?

III. The Empress, reversed:

She is regal, her hair richly oiled, her diadem savage, and she stands in some ancient torch-lit throne room, her hand raised imperiously, her throne unoccupied behind her. Kneeling before her, face fixed towards in love, fear and adoration is a naked man, a wrought-iron chained collar around his neck, his face back and arms blue with the tattooed signs of slavery.

Reversed here, the Empress is love, gone sour. Someone you used to love, but do not now. You gained money from them? As a result of the argument we already described?

You're terribly quiet. Well, let's say it's true. The Tarot does not lie.

Across to the eighth card, beneath it. Fortune. Luck. The things that fall to us.

Nine of Wands:

A circle of nine standing stones on a misty, grassy plain. They are ancient and battered. As you gaze at the card, it becomes apparent to you that a figure, wreathed in shadow, is approaching you in their midst. The figure seems to move on the card with an indefinable but growing threat, and fills you with a growing, creeping dread, as if she will climb out of the card and come for you.

Perhaps this is more properly the Nine of Stones, eh? Or even the Nine of Graves. Either way, in the eighth position, it is violence, and see how this is underlined by

XI. Strength:

A woman, body in profile. Her right arm is made of jointed metal, all pistons and carapace plates, glistening with oil, fastened to the stump of her shoulder with rivets and wires that creates raw welts in the flesh and bone to which they are anchored. She flexes the arm into a fist, and out of the corner of her eyes looks at you with a sort of satisfaction and something of menace.

Strength here? A Struggle. A fight.

Now, now. If you want to bring a knife here, if your hands carry the stains of blood that is not your own, yes, perhaps it's obvious I might say that. But you shuffled the cards, my love. You dealt them.

Now, now, sit back down, and yes, put the knife back there. For the reading has much to tell you, and we have barely begun.

The third position is the place of inspiration. Of ideas.

Here is a thing, here is

The Queen of Cups, reversed:

A woman, slim, dark-haired, stands in contrapposto on a pedestal, one breast exposed by her flimsy robe, a diadem on her brow. She holds a golden chalice overflowing with an opaque liquid of the deepest red. Her skin has a dull, waxy pallor.

The Queen of Cups is a lover. Reversed in this position, she tells us that — and this confirms what has gone before, doesn't it? — that she is not your lover any more.

You know that, I think. She covers

0. The Fool:

A rocky crag, silhouetted against the dawn or perhaps the dusk, yellow, pink, violet, and red, rich and bloody. A figure has leapt from the peak and is caught in midair, hands flailing towards the sun.

The fight. It wasn't a thing you thought through, was it? The ending of your love affair, I mean. You did it on impulse, acted on a gut feeling. That's what the Fool represents, an action unconsidered, and possibly, given context — the Tower, the Lovers — perverse, for the Fool is the eternal recusant, the droplet of water that refuses the ocean, and perversity is always part of the Fool's story.

What stands opposite? The ninth position speaks of contracts, agreements. Plans.

Seven of Pentacles:

A hand, its owner unseen, crafts with a knife or scalpel an intricate design onto a roundel made of some sort of pale-coloured leather or skin. Six more are pinned to the wall in the background, drying.

This is interesting. The seven normally denotes planning, craft, when all up to this point has given us an impulsive action. But here, we have the quintessential card of planning. Perhaps the card it covers will illuminate.

XVII. The Star:

A creature, gilled, fish-tailed, drags an ornate carved golden star down into the depths with clawed hands. As it retreats it stares at you with blank, milky round orbs that seem nonetheless loaded with malice.

Illuminate is what this card does by definition. You poured your soul into what you did, dreamed and plotted, festered, until one day you lashed out, is that correct? Still, the Tarot seems to be hostile to you this evening. Its images are moving against you.

Why is that, I wonder?

The fourth position, then. Security. The home.

Three of Wands, reversed:

Some winged creature of primeval nightmare, skin glistening and rubbery, squats across three crossed branches, its long beak-like snout open in some sort of cry, filled with dozens of needle-sharp teeth.

What you did, It removed any sense of safety you had. You feel ill at ease. I don't need to be a clairvoyant to work that out, dear. On the run, perhaps? It was hard for you, wasn't it? Ah, but how hard? Harder than anything, for here is

XII. The Hanged One:

A figure hangs upside-down, suspended by a web of cords, straps and chains attached to the body, wound tightly around chest, limbs and neck. Barbed hooks keep the body in suspension, pull the skin out of shape, like clay. The figure's mouth is open, wide eyes rolled back so the whites are mostly visible, and it is unclear whether this is due to pain or ecstasy. You shift in your seat at the thought of it, aware of the stickiness at your fingertips; no small part of your disquiet is due to the resemblance you perceive this figure as having to you, and the flutter of excitement in your stomach and between your legs as you find yourself wondering unbidden what it would be like to be tortured that way, and whether you might enjoy it.

This card shows that you have sacrificed everything that mattered to you. Do you care, though? Let's see. For in the tenth space is your honour. The result of your principles.

Four of Swords:

Four knives, very like the chef's knife that you placed on the table between you and the cards when you got here, hang from a rack on what could be a tomb.

The four in this position is a card that prefigures loneliness, seclusion from the world. Perhaps beneath it is the reason?

Why don't you lift the card?

Ah. There is a reason.

VIII. Justice:

A right hand holds a human heart, freshly cut out of its host, so fresh it seems almost to be beating still. Blood pools between the fingers; it runs down over the heel of the hand and trickles down the wrist in sticky, clotted rivulets. You can feel the stickiness on your own fingers, snd your stomach knots in fear, but not guilt, never guilt.

Justice. To be separated from the world by Justice? One might assume a sojourn at Her Majesty's Pleasure, perhaps? It would be easy to be so literal, but do you know, my dear, I think the Tarot has other surprises in store.

Part of you wants it, perhaps.

Already it is moving for you. Can you see it?

Of course you can. Here, here we see how it accommodates you, for here, in the fifth position, the position of things beginning, the Five of Cups has become the

Five of Wounds:

A woman's face, one you know, bearing an expression of comically dumb, open-mouthed surprise. A trickle of blood runs down between wide, unseeing eyes from one of five deep round wounds in her forehead. She — the she you wanted to know about when you came here — she had that expression, you recall, in the second before her body caught up with her brain and she slumped, already so very dead, to the floor. Those lifeless eyes, frozen in shock. Those eyes.

Self-explanatory, I think, and look, my darling, my beauty, no High Priestess lies underneath for you, oh no, your future has incurred the wrath of

136

II. The Revenant:

A figure sits at a table on which a bloodied chef's knife lies beneath a twelve-place Tarot spread. Behind the figure, a woman's corpse reaches out a hand as if to grasp the querent by the shoulder.

You feel a terrible cold prickling at the nape of your neck.

You will not look over your shoulder.

You will not.

You will not.

Stay seated. You have no choice, do you? You are the one who sees things through to the end, are you not? I think all three of us know that, don't we, my darling morsel?

Here, you can lift the eleventh card. It's the position of your desires.

Go on.

Three of Cups:

An indeterminate number of men and women, nude, shaven-headed, engage in a tangle of writhing limbs, gasping faces, in several varieties of sexual congress: genital, mouth, hand, orifice. Three hands protrude from the writing mass, holding cups, one of which collects blood and semen.

See, fulfilment. Catharsis. That's not so bad. It is what you wanted from the beginning, isn't it, my pretty? Release, without thought, or responsibility, or the burden of choice. But what sort of catharsis, hmm? What sort?

XV. The Devil:

The clairvoyant is laughing at you as you lift the Three to reveal a depiction of a figure, lion-headed, man-bodied, massively endowed, rests taloned hands on the shoulders of a young man and a young woman, both shackled around the neck. The man has his eyes closed, and bears an expression of resignation on his face. The woman, however, stares at you, pleading for help.

This sort of catharsis: self-destruction. Slavery. The surrender of your self to your appetites. You gave in long ago.

For see, my lovely, my morsel, it strikes me that you have already destroyed yourself with your crime.

You killed her. You killed her and oh your heart is full of guilt and shame and the knife lying there on the table in front of you with her blood going all black and sticky on its edge, that's just another reminder.

Oh dear, oh dear, oh dear. We are in a pickle, aren't we? Stare at the knife all you like, my pretty, but you and I both know it's staying on the table.

I think you know what's coming in the sixth position, the place of responsibility, of consequences. Of course you do. Here. Pick it up.

The Knight of Eyes:

A figure in clothes resembling yours, face ruined by bloody, empty sockets reaches out towards you plaintively, the eyes missing from the face in the palms of each hand.

Pentacles, Eyes. Valuable, see. Currency. Whoever has eyes to see, let them see, eh? Hah!

138

You came here for illumination, didn't you? You wanted to understand what you'd done. But the Tarot doesn't explain to you what you know already, and it's none of my business to know how or why you murdered your lover so brutally, so... messily. I don't want to know.

Pick it up. Don't be shy now.

XIII. Death:

Skull-faced, in jeans and a T-shirt, the Reaper stands over an open, shallow grave shovelling earth in. A hand reaches from the grave, pleading, begging succour. No sympathy is given.

Of course it's Death! What else could it be? The irony is of course that this is one of the most benign cards you've dealt yourself, for it is the card of endings, of the finish. It tells us that it will be over soon, my pretty.

Only one spot to go, the twelfth, for the unexpected, for the outside influence, for the secret ending. And look! Oh, look! My Tarot has outdone itself for you. A Queen of Swords is your nemesis, but here, for you, it has become

The Queen of Books:

A woman of stately age and impressive girth, grey curly hair framing a round, hard face with eyes so blue that they bore into you, triumphantly. She sits on the opposite side of the table, a twelve-place spread of the Tarot between you. On the near side of the table, the bloodied chef's knife, and a pair of hands spotted with blood, as your own, resting on the baize. The twelfth card in the pictured reading duplicates this card,

139

and you know that if you stare hard enough, you will fall into it, into an infinite recursion, forever.

What sword bites as comprehensively as a book? And the Tarot, why, I told you at the beginning that the Tarot is the Book of Thoth, the infinite repository of divinatory wisdom. It is itself the Queen of Books, and as the Queen of Books, my dear, my darling, my lovely, my beauty, it is your nemesis.

Here we are. You sought refuge, but the Tarot offers no refuge for such as you, with your threats and the blood on your knife and the blood on your hands, only truth.

If you are sincere with the Tarot, the Tarot will be sincere with you. Didn't I say? It is being sincere with you.

One last card, then. One final card to finish you off.

XX. The Reckoning:

You — it's you, it was always you — sit by the window of the room, clutching at your throat, eyes bulging, as the spectre of your murdered lover, butchered, a walking corpse, stands behind you, hands tight around your throat, calmly strangling you. You try to scramble for the knife, look up at the smiling clairvoyant, but you already feel the cold fingers at your neck, so cold they burn your skin. In the picture on the card, the world outside the window explodes in mushroom clouds and fire. An apocalypse, the end of everything.

29266256R00081

Printed in Poland
by Amazon Fulfillment
Poland Sp. z o.o., Wrocław